Learning to Love

~ SAUL'S STORY ~

J. E. B. Spredemann

Blessed Publishing

Published in Indiana by Blessed Publishing.

www.jebspredemann.com

Cover design by J.E.B. Spredemann

BOOKS BY J.E.B. SPREDEMANN
(*J. Spredemann)

AMISH GIRLS SERIES

Joanna's Struggle

Danika's Journey

Chloe's Revelation

Susanna's Surprise

Annie's Decision

Abigail's Triumph

Brooke's Quest

Leah's Legacy

NOVELLAS*

*Amish by Accident**

An Unforgivable Secret – Amish Secrets 1*

A Secret Encounter – Amish Secrets 2*

A Secret of the Heart – Amish Secrets 3*

Learning to Love – Saul's Story (Sequel to
Chloe's Revelation – adult novella)*

A Christmas of Mercy – Amish Girls Holiday

NOVELETTES*

Cindy's Story – *An Amish Fairly Tale Novelette 1*
Rosabelle's Story – *An Amish Fairly Tale Novelette 2*

COMING SOON! (Lord Willing)

Amish Fairly Tales (title not yet available) – *Amish Secrets 4, prequel to Amish by Accident*

For My Mom

Words cannot express how much you mean to me.
Thank you for everything. I love you.

Author's Note

It should be noted that the Amish people and their communities differ one from another. There are, in fact, no two Amish communities exactly alike. It is this premise on which this book is written. We have taken cautious steps to assure the authenticity of Amish practices and customs. Both Old Order Amish and New Order Amish are portrayed in this work of fiction and may be inconsistent with some Amish communities.

We, as *Englischers*, can learn a lot from the Plain People and their simple way of life. Their hard work, close-knit family life, and concern for others are to be applauded. As the Lord wills, may this special culture continue to be respected and remain so for many centuries to come, and may the light of God's salvation reach their hearts.

Characters in *Saul's Story*

The Brenneman Family
Saul – protagonist
Sarah – protagonist
Eb – Saul's father
Salome – Saul's mother

The Mast Family
Bishop Mast – Sarah's father
Judy – Sarah's sister

The Fisher Family
Jonathan – prominent character throughout the Amish Girls Series

The Hostettler Family
Judah – Bishop of Paradise and other nearby districts
Levi – Judah's son, Chloe's husband
Chloe – Levi's wife, protagonist of Chloe's Revelation
Hannah – Levi and Chloe's four-year-old daughter
Lydia (Lyddie) – Levi and Chloe's two-year-old daughter

Others
Truda – Englisch friend of Sarah
Stephen Esh – Chloe's older brother
Ruthie Esh – Chloe's younger sister
Ethan Spencer – Ruthie's betrothed

Characters in *Saul's Story* (Cont.)

Danika Yoder – Chloe's friend, protagonist of Danika's Journey, herbalist

Joanna Scott – Chloe's friend, protagonist of Joanna's Struggle

Unofficial Glossary
of Pennsylvania Dutch Words

Ach – Oh

Appeditlich – Delicious

Ausbund – Amish hymn book

Bloobier – Blueberry

Boppli – Baby

Bopplin – Babies

Bruder – Brother

Dat, Daed – Dad

Dawdi – Grandfather

Denki – Thanks

Der Herr – The Lord

Dochder – Daughter

Dokter – Doctor

Dummkopp – Dummy

Elbedritschel – Small mythical animal

Englischer – A non-Amish person

Ferhoodled – Mixed up, Crazy

Fraa – Woman, Wife

Gott – God

Gut – Good

Guten Mayrie – Good Morning

Haus – House

Hiya – Hi

Hullo – Hello

Jah – Yes

Kapp – Prayer Covering

Kline Bischen – Little bit

Kumm – Come

Lieb – Love

Liede – Song

Mamm – Mom

Mammi – Grandmother

Mei Lieb – My Love

Mein Liewe – My Dear

Mudder – Mother

Nee – No

Ordnung – Rules of the Amish Community

Rumspringa – Running around years

Schweschder – Sister

Vadder – Father

Vorsinger – Song Leader

Wilkom – Welcome

Wunderbaar – Wonderful

A brief summary of *Chloe's Revelation (Amish Girls Series – Book 3)*, the prequel to **Learning to Love - Saul's Story...**

Chloe Esh has been the apple of Levi Hostettler's eye for many years, unbeknownst to her. Timid Levi nearly loses his chance to court Chloe when Saul Brenneman, from a neighboring district, asks to drive Chloe home from a Singing. Chloe falls in love with handsome Saul and the two of them make plans for a future together until Saul discovers Bishop Mast's daughter, Sarah, is in the family way, allegedly with Saul's *boppli*. With a heavy heart, Saul breaks things off with Chloe and she finds love again with Levi Hostettler. Saul Brenneman regretfully agrees to marry Sarah Mast. Thus, the beginning of *Learning to Love – Saul's Story*.

PROLOGUE

*H*ot tears streamed down Saul Brenneman's face as he rode his Appaloosa through the shadowy woodland. He could hardly bear to see Chloe's breaking heart, so much like his own. To tell the woman he loved – the woman he'd pledged to spend the rest of his life with – that he must leave her for another, had been a load too heavy to bear. Oh, how he loathed himself on this dreadful night!

So many thoughts had swirled through his mind; surely there was a way to work this out...*Chloe and I could run away together and marry. No, we'd both be shunned and cut off from our families. Maybe Sarah could go to one of those homes for unwed mothers and then give the baby up for adoption. No, Chloe might not even want me after finding out what I've done. Perhaps if Chloe were in the family way too... No, then Chloe would surely be shamed in her community. Dummkopp*, he chided himself incredulously for that last sinful thought. Truly he was desperate and not thinking clearly. In the end, he'd chosen to take responsibility for his actions and do what was expected of him – the right thing.

All he knew now is that he must pull himself together, because tomorrow was his wedding day…whether he liked it or not.

ONE

Just breathe, Saul told himself.

As the *Vorsinger* led out in song, Saul was reminded of their ancestral saints that had gone before their People. It was a last song, a song of death. Slow, mournful. That's precisely how Saul was feeling at this very moment. Like dying. Like running back to Chloe, begging her forgiveness, and carrying her away to some far-away land where they could live happily ever after. Isn't that how it's supposed to happen?

Instead, he sat across from Sarah Mast, the bishop's daughter. He only half-listened to the short sermon the ministers preached about married couples throughout the Bible. This wasn't a normal wedding ceremony by any means. Sarah and her mother hadn't planted any celery in anticipation of it. They didn't invite their many hundreds of friends and family members. They wouldn't go out to the homes of friends and loved ones to collect gifts for their home. In fact, the only thing normal about this wedding was that it was after the harvest – well, the early harvest – barely.

The sound of Sarah's sniffling seemed to pound in his ears. He didn't dare look up. He, too, brushed away a tear, but his was a tear of frustration. Wasn't there a logical way out of this mess? His heartbeat quickened by the second. This was really going to happen.

He'd noticed earlier that Sarah was now showing. Their sinful deed evident for all to see. He sighed. He'd never imagined himself married at seventeen...and expecting a *boppli*. Heat rose up his neck and he could feel the perspiration bead on his forehead.

What was supposed to be the happiest day of his life had turned into the most horrific. So many times he'd imagined this day with Chloe by his side. He would lock eyes with her and they'd silently communicate their love for one another before a vow was even spoken. When the proper time came, he would take her hand and, with all his heart, repeat the vows the bishop spoke. Then he'd take her home and share all the love he'd kept bottled up inside. He'd pictured them blissfully married in their own little farmhouse with *kinner* galore all around them as a testament of their love. A happy life...a perfect life.

But now that would never be.

No. Instead he was stuck with Sarah Mast all his days. And despite his previous desire to court her, he now only held contempt in his heart toward her. After all, this was just as much her fault as it was his own. Why hadn't she protested? Why hadn't she stopped them from sinning? Didn't women know when they would conceive? Another thought occurred to him: *did she become pregnant on purpose?*

4

Saul allowed his thoughts to wander back to that fateful night. He had been the one to suggest they go to his *Englisch* friends' party. It wasn't the first one he'd been to. He and a couple of Amish buddies had been before and he enjoyed the company of his *Englisch* friends. But he'd never drunk as much alcohol as he had when Sarah was with him that night.

It hadn't been her first party either. He'd seen her at one of the hoedowns Zeke Eicher had held in his parents' barn when they were out of state visiting relatives. He wished he could remember what exactly happened that night, but somehow the alcohol had erased a portion of his memory, leaving a thick fog in its place. He now wondered just how much Sarah recalled.

Thoughts whirled in his mind. The last thing he could remember was his *Englisch* friends encouraging him to drink another beer...or was it a shot of something stronger? His next recollection was waking up in a strange bedroom with a disheveled Sarah Mast at his side. Instantly, he'd realized what they'd done. And immediately he regretted it. He'd always intended to wait until his wedding day. He'd wanted to give himself away to the woman he loved. He hadn't known it then, but he realized now it was Chloe he'd been waiting for. He'd given his most special, sacred gift to someone he didn't even care for.

Oh God, Saul prayed, *what have I done*? He'd give anything...*anything* to go back and erase that night.

"Saul Brenneman!"

Saul blinked back to the present at the snap of Bishop Mast's fingers and frustrated tone of voice. He looked over and saw

Sarah standing and knew he was supposed to be standing next to her with their hands joined. Saul lifted his weight from the chair and forced himself to stand in front of the bishop, but he could not take Sarah's hand.

"Join hands," the bishop calmly pronounced the command that shouldn't have been necessary.

Saul stood in defiance, hands clenched at his side. The minister walked over and placed Sarah's hand in Saul's. He allowed her to loosely grasp his limp hand. Her small hand felt clammy and Saul realized she must be nervous too.

The bishop spoke the words – marriage vows – to which he was to agree to. Saul forced himself to say, "*Jah*," because that was what he had to do, but he knew it was a lie.

Sarah walked into the small *dawdi haus* on her father's property, just a few hundred feet from the main dwelling. Normally the small cottage, intended for grandparents, would be attached to the main dwelling, but outlying buildings made its proximity impossible. Sarah sat a box of linens down on the small oak dining table and wondered how long she and Saul would live with her folks. Would she ever have her own house, the home she'd always dreamed of as a little girl?

She felt a sudden movement from inside her belly and rubbed where the little one made its presence known. Only a slight smile tipped the corner of her mouth. Was the *boppli* a *bu* or a *maedel*? She wondered if it would make a difference as far as Saul was concerned. Probably not. One thing she was certain of, though. She would not ask his opinion. As much as she could, she determined to stay out of Saul's path and let him deal with things his own way. He was clearly still in shock, whereas she'd already had several months to come to terms with her reality – not that it had been easy. No, far from it.

Sarah's eyes scanned the pots and casserole dishes that lined the small countertop, thankful that some of the community members had brought meals. The last thing she felt like doing was cooking after that whole shameful wedding ordeal. Couldn't Saul just pretend he cared for her and their *boppli* a little?

Heavy footsteps drew her attention to the back door. Saul. She sighed, then turned back to her box of linens to keep her hands busy. She walked to a small pantry and placed some folded hand towels on one of the shelves. The *dawdi haus* was pretty much prepared for them already, but Sarah wanted to add a few items she had kept in her dower chest.

Saul slowly opened the creaking door, letting it slam shut behind him. Sarah winced as he seemed to drag his feet across the floor. He sat down at the table with a thud and covered his face with his hands. Sarah was unsure what to do. Should she attempt to comfort him?

"Would you like something to eat?" Her voice sounded quiet even to herself and she was unsure if Saul had even heard the words.

Silence.

"*Jah, kline bischen*," he eventually answered.

Good. At least she would have something to occupy her mind, distracting her from a grumpy husband. *Husband.* She sighed again.

Saul must've heard the burdened breath escape her lips. "You know, if it's too much trouble I can get it myself," he spoke the words with an edge of frustration.

"*Nee.* I...I'm just tired is all." Sarah's hands shook slightly as she swiftly removed a bowl from the cupboard, filled it with the chicken soup her aunt had made, and cut a thick slice of her mamm's homemade bread. She set it on the table in front of him and then fetched a glass of tea.

Sarah then made quick work of the meals on the counter, placing them into the refrigerator. "I'm going to lie down now... uh, if you don't mind."

Saul nodded in silence.

Nearing the only bedroom in the small house, Sarah thought of their sleeping arrangements. It would be strange to sleep next to a man for the first time. Of course, technically it wasn't the first time, but she didn't remember much of the actual first time. That was how they got into this predicament in the first place. Surely Saul wouldn't expect anything from her now that they were husband and wife, would he? No, she was certain Saul had no desire to be near *her.* His heart clearly belonged to another.

Sarah pulled the bedding back and slipped in between the coarse sheets. Her bulky body coiled into the fetal position and she began to sob. She placed a hand over her protruding abdomen and gently rubbed where the baby had just kicked. "I'm sorry, little one. I'm sorry for bringing you into a home without love."

Although he knew the chicken soup was probably delicious, Saul could barely stomach a few bites. A heavy weight settled on his shoulders. He couldn't do this. This burden was too much.

Okay, Lord. I know I was stupid. But why? Why did you have to allow Sarah to get pregnant? Why did you let me fall in love with Chloe? My heart longs for her, Lord. I can't love Sarah. I have nothing to give her. My heart belongs to Chloe; I know it always will. Will my whole existence consist of what once was, what I'll never have again? Oh God, can anything stop this aching in my heart?

You know my thoughts, God. You know that when I look at Sarah, I'm reminded of all I've lost. I know it's not right but I despise her, Lord. She and the boppli *she carries are the reason I can't be with Chloe. They've stolen my happiness. I don't know if I can do this. Lord, help me to see my way through.*

Saul sprung up from the table and dumped the remaining soup from his bowl into the trash can. He walked to the door and peered out the back window. It wasn't quite dusk yet. There was still time. He hurried to the small living room and quickly unbuttoned the *for-gut* vest he'd worn to his wedding ceremony and tossed it onto the couch. He grabbed his straw hat and headed to the barn to saddle his horse.

As Saul mounted the large animal, Bishop Mast emerged from one of the darkened stalls. "Going somewhere?" The bishop raised his eyebrows.

"*Jah*. Out. I need some fresh air." Saul brushed his father-in-law off. He clucked his tongue, turned the horse around, and raced off at an unsafe speed.

He didn't know where he was going. He just knew that he couldn't stay there. He gave the mare her head and basked in the cool air indicative of an early fall evening. Allowing his horse to lead the way, he closed his eyes. When he opened them again, he realized the mare was headed toward the Esh farm. So be it. He didn't redirect the animal, but allowed her to crest the hill of the Esh property line then brought her to a halt.

Saul sat atop the horse and watched through a thicket of trees. It had been these very woods where he'd proposed to Chloe and she'd said yes. It was a promise he'd never intended – never wanted – to break. He would have married her that day if he could.

He didn't know how long he'd been there, but the surrounding terrain had darkened significantly. He scanned the perimeter of the house. No sign of his beloved. Was she inside still lamenting for him? Should he go to her window and throw a pebble to summon her? And then what? It wasn't as though he could call her down and hold her in his arms.

He was married now. His heavy shoulders rose and fell.

A twig snapped behind him. He listened intently, but didn't turn around. Saul stood still and silent in case a wild animal was prowling nearby. He chided himself for failing to bring protection. Of course, he really didn't have a plan when he first set out.

If he lost his life now, would it really be so bad? What did he have worth living for?

When all was silent again, Saul circumspectly turned the horse around. A bright light suddenly shined in his eyes, and he was nearly blinded. Now he did feel like Saul of Tarsus, as Chloe's little sister Ruthie had once called him. He instinctively covered his eyes.

"What are you doing here?" a brusque voice sounded behind the stream of brightness.

Saul breathed a sigh of relief. *Chloe's brother.* "Stephen. You startled me."

"You're not welcome here anymore, Saul." Stephen finally lowered the flashlight. "Shouldn't you be home with your *fraa*? And *boppli*? That's what happened, right? You left Chloe because you had another *maedel* back home?"

Saul grimaced. "That's not how it was. I loved Chloe. I *still* love her." He didn't appreciate Stephen's accusatory tone, but what could he say? He'd made a foolish mistake that cost him everything.

"Yeah, that's about right. Cheating two women," Stephen said wryly. "You certainly don't deserve my sister."

Saul clenched his fists. "I don't have to stand for this," he said through gritted teeth.

"Seems to me you don't stand for much of anything," he spewed.

Saul clicked his tongue and tugged on the reins. He needed to get out of there before he did or said something uncharitable. While he understood Stephen's point of view, he did not appreciate his underhanded insults. *I guess I should get used to comments like that.*

TWO

*A*ll eyes turned to Sarah as she entered her childhood home. *Dat, Mamm,* and her three younger siblings sat at the breakfast table enjoying their morning meal. Sarah hadn't eaten anything. Oh, how she wished she was still here in this house with her family, surrounded by love. But she knew life would never be the same.

Now, every time she entered her folks' place she was reminded of her failures. Telling her father, the bishop of their district, that she was in the family way had been the most difficult thing she'd ever done. He didn't treat her any differently, but the disappointment and shame was written all over his face. She'd heard the unspoken words loud and clear. *I'm ashamed of you,* dochder. *Don't you realize how this makes our family look? How will those in our community come to me for guidance when I can't even guide my own house properly? How can I expect the People to follow God's Word when my own* dochder *refuses to? You have disrespected me.*

Tears now pricked her eyes. "*Dat,* I need to speak with you."

Bishop Mast nodded, placed his paper towel on the table, and arose from his chair. "Let us go outside."

Sarah followed her father out the back door. They sat side by side on the porch swing, gently swaying. "I'm worried about Saul, *Dat*. He left the night we married and he still hasn't returned. It's been four days."

"He did not mention where he was going?"

"*Nee*. Do you think he has gone back to Bishop Hostettler's district?" What she meant was *did he leave me and go back to Chloe*? Those words were too difficult to say, though.

"You must pray for him, Sarah. I cannot bring Saul back." He sighed. "And I cannot make him love you."

Sarah's chin quivered. "I know. I'm so sorry, *Dat*. I'm sorry I disappointed you."

Bishop Mast place his arm around his daughter's shoulder. "You will get through this, Sarah. *Der Herr* will help you. Saul just needs time. He is a *gut* man. He will be a *gut* father to your *kinner*."

She swiped a tear. "I hope you are right, *Dat*."

"Sarah, nobody enters marriage knowing what to do. Everyone starts off the same way. When two people marry, they are as strangers. As you and Saul spend time together and get to know each other, that is when the feeling of love comes. But beware: the feeling of love comes and goes. It is not constant. True love is basically just a promise of hope. Hope that you will learn how to dwell together in unity. It is a commitment to meet one another's needs. *Die Bibel* says it does not seek its own, it is kind, it does not envy, it does not think evil, it bears all things. We must strive for these things and more. Love is a never-ending learning process."

Sarah nodded meekly. "I will strive to love Saul according to the Bible, but I fear he will not return my love."

"Remember, it does not seek its own. It is hardest to give when we do not receive anything in return." He squeezed her hand. "But *Der Herr* says that our labor is not is vain. He will be your reward. Cling to that, Sarah."

The clip-clop of horse hooves drew their attention toward the barn. Bishop Mast arose from the swing. "It appears the prodigal has come home. He will probably appreciate a *gut* meal, *jah?*"

"*Jah.*" Sarah gave her father a half-smile. "Please pray for us, *Dat.*"

"Oh, I have been," he assured. "And I will continue."

"*Denki.*" Sarah descended the porch steps and hurried to the *dawdi haus*, hoping to arrive before Saul did.

Saul dismounted his horse and brought her to a tub of water to drink. He wearily led her to a stall in the barn and forked some fresh alfalfa for her enjoyment. Although he should properly care for his mare and give her a good brushing, he was simply too exhausted. A shower, a hot meal, and a bed was what he needed.

Trudging into the kitchen, the scent of beef stew tantalized Saul's nostrils. He glanced around, but Sarah appeared to be nowhere in sight. *Does she know I'm home, or did she prepare this for herself?* He eyed the small pot speculating whether or not he should indulge, until he spied a single ceramic bowl on the table.

"Sarah?" he called out, not endeavoring to enter the bedroom.

His *fraa* appeared around the corner. "Oh, um...are you hungry? I fixed some stew leftover from last night."

Guilt nibbled at Saul. Had she waited each night, expecting him to return? *"Jah,* I'm starving, actually."

"I saw ya comin' so I put it on for you. I thought maybe you'd be wantin' something." She stared at her hands as though they should be doing something. Sarah quickly walked over to the stove. "Do you want to take a shower first?"

Did he smell that bad? Probably, but he didn't think he possessed the strength to stand for another minute without nourishment. *"Nee,* I should probably eat. I'm quite exhausted. I'll shower later."

Sarah promptly brought the pot to the table and Saul took a seat as she ladled out a bowlful of stew.

Saul swallowed hard as she ministered to him and nodded in appreciation. He bowed his head in silent prayer, then quickly devoured his meal. It was certainly one of the best he'd ever tasted. After all, he hadn't eaten much of anything, aside from a few plants and such he'd found out in the wild, in days.

Sarah sat in the wooden rocker in the *schtupp* and tapped her toe, waiting for Saul to emerge from the bathroom. She'd planned to keep silent and let Saul's disappearance slide, but she couldn't stand the thought of her husband going off to see another woman, *if* that was indeed where he'd gone. Had he been with his beloved Chloe the entire four days he'd been absent? Sarah's thoughts ran rampant, imagining every possible detrimental outcome. She hadn't said anything while he ate, giving him a chance to relax from wherever he'd been, but now she needed some answers.

This marriage certainly wasn't an ideal situation for either of them, but she was willing to make it work. After all, it wasn't just the two of them. They had a little one to think about.

The moment Saul emerged from the restroom, she was reminded why she'd been attracted to him in the first place. His dark hair, now damp and tousled, contrasted nicely with his deep blue eyes. And he hadn't shaved – a sign that he belonged to her. The dark stubble on his face matched the hair on his head and Sarah found herself involuntarily drawn to his masculine presence.

"I'm tired." He glanced down at the couch.

That's when Sarah noticed his attire – boxer shorts and a t-shirt. *Oh boy.* Pink immediately tinted her ivory cheeks.

Saul frowned. "Where are the blankets?"

"Oh, they're in the closet. I can get one for you." Sarah hurried to the bedroom and fetched a blanket and the pillow from his side of the bed. She'd hoped that perhaps...no, it was foolish to think he'd want to sleep in the same bed. She handed the items to Saul, wanting to offer him half of their bed, but kept silent instead.

Saul spread out the blanket and plopped down onto the couch.

Sarah watched as he closed his eyes and began snoring less than a minute later. She sighed. *I guess I'll have to wait until tomorrow to talk to him.*

Sarah had a difficult time falling asleep. Thoughts seemed to ping pong in her mind. One minute, she thought of Saul going to see Chloe and she'd stew in resentment. The next, she envisioned him emerging from the bathroom in his boxer shorts and messed hair and her heart filled with desire. But not just a physical desire – a longing to be loved. She yearned to see Saul's face radiate with joy as it had the months prior to their wedding, when he thought he'd be spending the rest of his life with someone he actually loved – *Chloe*.

Eventually, Sarah drifted off to sleep, but she found no solace. Nothing she did could satisfy the unrequited longing in her heart, nor appease a husband whose heart clearly belonged to someone else.

THREE

*S*aul breathed in the welcome scent of coffee and slowly sipped on the steaming beverage as Sarah prepared breakfast. He'd slept better than he had in a while, even though the couch was too short for his long legs. After spending four days out in the elements, nearly anything would have sufficed.

He wasn't sure if he'd accomplished anything at all out there, but sheer exhaustion compelled him to return home. *Home?* This tiny place certainly didn't feel like home, but it's what he'd earned, he reckoned. *Stephen was probably right, I don't deserve Chloe.*

Sarah sat a pot of oatmeal on the table, with freshly buttered toast, and sat down. Saul bowed his head and offered a silent prayer for the meal and the roof over his head. That was all he could manage for now.

He dished out some oatmeal, added a dab of butter, brown sugar, and milk, mixed it up, and then took a bite. Saul savored the delicious flavors as they mingled together. He glanced up to see Sarah frowning, an empty bowl in front of her, and he wondered if perhaps he'd forgotten something.

"What's wrong?" he asked, eyeing her bowl.

Sarah's eyes met his and held a steady gaze. "Where did you go, Saul? Where have you been the last four days?"

"That's none of your concern." Saul grimaced and shoved another spoonful of oatmeal into his mouth.

"Did you go to see *her*?"

Saul didn't appreciate her tone; he was the head of this house. "I said it's none of your concern."

"Yes, it is my concern. I'm supposed to be *your wife*, remember? I think I have a right to know where my husband's been."

"Yes, I went to see *Chloe*." He glared at Sarah and stood up from the table, his chair screeched on the wooden floor. "And I'll go see her again if I want to. I didn't ask for this marriage."

Saul noticed tears in Sarah's eyes. "I didn't ask for it either! But we're both stuck with each other whether we like it or not."

"Yeah right. I was the one that had too much to drink that night. I'm quite certain you knew exactly what you were doing. I bet you planned this!"

Sarah's mouth fell open. "I *planned* this? You...you think *I*, the *bishop's* daughter, *wanted* to become pregnant out of wedlock?"

Now that she put it that way, it did sound kind of silly, he admitted.

She continued, "I was just as out of it as you were, Saul. You're the one who took me to the party! Don't you dare go blaming me. And if you want to know the truth, right now I'd rather be married to *anyone* but you!"

Saul quickly moved to the back door and lifted his hat from the peg. "This is ridiculous. I'm going to work. I'll be back at suppertime. *Maybe*." He walked out the back door and let it slam behind him.

Sarah buried her face in her hands and sobbed. That was not how the conversation was supposed to turn out. Instead of solving their problems, she'd just made matters worse by provoking Saul to wrath. And she couldn't believe he accused *her* of planning this. She should have just kept her mouth closed. What would supper be like tonight...and for the rest of their lives?

Eb Brenneman watched from the woodworking shop as his son drove up in his buggy. He hadn't seen Saul since the wedding, although his *fraa* had urged him to visit. Eb thought it would be better to give the young couple time to adjust to each other, but by the look on his son's face, it didn't seem as though he'd adjusted all that well yet.

"Good morning, *sohn*."

Saul's frown didn't budge. "Hey, *Dat*."

His son's somber tone gave him pause for concern. This was not the Saul he knew. A couple months ago it seemed as though nothing could steal his joy. Now he clearly battled some internal darkness. Unfortunately, Eb knew there was little he could do to ease his son's melancholy. "Would you like to talk?"

"*Nee*. I've had enough talking for one day. Let's just work."

Eb sighed. "If that's what you'd like, *sohn*."

Saul picked up his tool belt and fastened it to his waist. "*Jah*, that's what I'd like."

"Would you mind if your old *daed* offered you a bit of advice?"

Saul shrugged half-heartedly and sighed.

"I know your heart is still aching over a certain *maedel*. And perhaps you are not getting along so well with your new *fraa*? Sometimes we're dealt hard things in life, but we've got to make the best of it. That's all we can do. You have a choice: you can gripe and complain about your lot and carry bitterness around every day of your life, or you can accept it, determine to make the most of it, and possibly find happiness. But the choice is yours. Nobody can make it for you. If you're always looking back at what you've lost, you'll never discover the treasure that lies just up ahead."

Saul didn't respond, but at least he appeared to have been listening.

Eb worked alongside Saul all day with nary a word about his home life. Eb hoped his son was contemplating the advice he'd given. Work orders for current and potential customers were discussed, along with the weather and talk of his siblings' families. Eb looked forward to the day when Saul would be excited about building a play structure for his own *kinner*. As of now, Eb worried about this first *grossboppli* Saul's wife would be having. If there were problems at home and it was affecting Saul this much, the added stress certainly couldn't be good for the baby.

"Your mother and I would like to join you for supper sometime," Eb said.

Saul's face brightened a little and it lifted Eb's spirits knowing his son desired their company. "*Jah*. That sounds *gut*. Tomorrow should be fine."

Eb's brow lifted. "Tomorrow? It wonders me if maybe you'd like to discuss it with your *fraa* first?"

Saul shrugged. "*Nee*. She'll probably be glad of it."

"All right, then, *sohn*. Tomorrow night it is. I'll let your *mamm* know. She'll be glad."

Sarah enjoyed the feel of the warm soapy water on her hands while she washed the supper dishes. Somehow it conveyed a comfort she hadn't experienced in quite a while. She recalled the innumerable times with her mother and sisters when they would all be working in the kitchen simultaneously. Oh, what fun they'd had! *Mamm* was usually teaching one of the younger *kinner* to bake whoopie pies or how to knead dough, while the older girls washed dishes, cleaned counters, filled lamps, or performed some other miscellaneous chore.

But Sarah remembered well, when she'd been one of the little ones. It seemed as though time stood still in those moments, yet it managed to zoom by. But it never seemed like work; it was simply cherished time spent together – memories that she valued even more, now that she was grown.

The *boppli* moved inside her womb and she lovingly placed her hand over her abdomen. Did she carry a little girl? Perhaps someone whom she could pass on the art of homemaking to? Would the two of them spend countless hours together providing love and nourishment for their family?

Sarah turned from the sink and caught Saul analyzing her from the entryway to the small living room. Sarah groaned inwardly. Oh no, not another argument. "Did you want to say something, Saul?" She hoped it would be an improvement over the silent supper they'd just shared.

"*Jah.* I thought you'd like to know that I invited my folks over for supper tomorrow night," he said casually.

Sarah's jaw dropped as she thought of all the preparations she'd have to make between now and then, along with fixing the meal. She quickly recovered and glanced into the refrigerator to see what she had on hand. "I don't have anything appropriate to make a proper meal for guests. And your folks, nonetheless."

"You can go shopping tomorrow morning. I have money in my wallet on the table; go ahead and take what you need." He scratched his head. "I'm gonna take a shower now."

After Saul disappeared into the bathroom, Sarah found his wallet on the small table in the *schtupp*. She opened it, feeling somewhat odd, as though she were intruding, and counted out a large stack of bills. *Does he always carry around this much money?* She took a few bills from the stack and slipped the remainder back into the wallet, when something caught her eye.

She reached into the wallet and pulled out a folded strip of smooth thick paper – photograph paper. Sarah unfolded the strip to reveal Saul and another girl – Chloe, she presumed – in four small black and white photos. She couldn't be sure it was Chloe because she'd never seen her. *No, while Saul was happily courting another* maedel, *I was home sick. And praying I wasn't in the family way*, she thought with a tinge of bitterness.

She glanced down at each photo and marveled at how happy the young couple seemed. Sarah frowned. *Nothing like us.* Saul was even brazenly planting a kiss on the girl's cheek in one of the photographs. She flipped the strip over and read, in Saul's handwriting: Ocean City with Chloe. He shouldn't have this, it's a graven image. But Sarah couldn't determine whether her righteous indignation was a result of the photo, or jealousy over Saul's adoration for Chloe. Probably the latter.

"What are you doing?" Saul's rough voice called from over her shoulder.

Sarah swallowed and her cheeks immediately reddened. She glanced down at the photographs she was still holding. "Oh, I...uh..."

Saul snatched the strip of photos from her hand, quickly refolded them, and shoved them back into his wallet. "You had no right to go nosing through my stuff, Sarah."

"You shouldn't have that. It's a graven image," she voiced her thoughts.

Saul's face darkened, but not from embarrassment. "Don't you start telling me what I should and shouldn't do. I don't ever want you going through my things again. Do you understand?"

Tears stung Sarah's eyes and she ran from the room.

Saul winced as he heard the door to the bedroom slam. He didn't take pleasure in making Sarah cry, but she needed to learn her place. And that didn't include sifting through his personal belongings. He sighed and plopped down onto the sofa. Opening his wallet, he pulled out the only memento he had left from his and Chloe's relationship. He gazed fondly at Chloe's bright smile, such a contrast from how he'd last seen her when tears flowed down her cheeks like a river.

He brought the photo to his heart and closed his eyes. *Oh, how I miss you, Chloe.*

"Saul?"

Saul shot up at the sound of Sarah's voice. Had he fallen asleep? He looked up at Sarah, the photo strip still pasted to his chest, a quizzical look on his brow. "*Jah?*"

"Oh, I didn't realize you were already asleep." Sarah diverted her gaze away from the photo, but Saul still caught the hurt on her face. She swallowed. "Before I go to bed, I just wanted to say I'm sorry. I…I've been praying and God showed me that I was wrong."

Saul blinked as though trying to comprehend what she'd just said. "You're sorry?"

"*Jah*. Will you forgive me?" She twisted her hands together. This clearly wasn't the easiest thing for her to do.

"Okay." It was all he could manage right now.

She nodded once. "Okay, good night." Sarah turned to walk back to the bedroom.

"Sarah, wait." Saul stood from the couch, tossing the photo strip near his wallet on the table. He walked over to his wife, who appeared confused by his proximity. He reached up and caressed a strand of her long hair that flowed down her back over her night dress.

"*Jah?*" Sarah gulped.

He noticed the longing in Sarah's eyes. Should he offer a token of peace?

"Thank you." Saul took a step closer, pulled her near, and pressed his lips to hers. It felt good to hold someone in his arms again.

Sarah's body and mind seemed to conflict, because Saul was certain she kissed him back. He knew she wanted him. But now she reluctantly pushed away. "No, Saul. I don't want you like this."

Now Saul was the one *ferhoodled*. "What do you mean?"

"I won't take your body without your soul." She placed her hand over her heart. "I want you here. I need all of you."

Saul followed Sarah's gaze to the photos on the table and watched as her eyes filled with tears.

"Good night, Saul," Sarah's voice shook as she spoke the words. She walked out of the living room where Saul stood dumbfounded.

What did I do wrong? Saul sighed. *I don't think I'll ever understand women.*

Sarah was now thoroughly confused. Saul had finally shown her affection – kissed her nonetheless – but the fact that it hadn't been out of love grieved her heart. She'd been yearning for his kiss, for his touch, but that wasn't the way it was supposed to happen.

She'd been reading the love chapter in her Bible, an English Bible that she would probably be reprimanded for, if it were ever discovered. But she craved truth, and her German wasn't too great, so she was willing to take the risk. An Amish-turned-*Englisch* young woman had given it to her.

She thought of the kind lady, Truda was her name, and the words she had spoken to her. Truda said that someone had shown her the truth and she now knew that you didn't have to be Amish to get to Heaven. These new thoughts confused Sarah. Her *dat*, the bishop no less, had always preached what their forefathers taught. She'd been warned, along with the others in their district, that if she ever left the Amish church and went against their *Ordnung* that she would be turned over to Satan. And if she never repented and rejoined the church, the lake of fire would most certainly be her home for all eternity. The only way she could possibly have hope of Heaven is to remain Amish all her days and do the best she could to live a righteous life. These thoughts had frightened her for sure and for certain.

But Truda said that the Bible taught something different. Sarah had never been allowed to read the Bible on her own. Her *vadder* and the other leaders warned that when one began studying the Bible, they would get crazy ideas. These crazy ideas would certainly take them away from the church and doom them to Hell. Sarah determined that she would find out the truth. What did God have to say? Truda agreed to meet with her privately to study God's Word, but she encouraged Sarah to read the Bible on her own and ask God to reveal His truth to her. And that's what she'd been doing lately.

She'd told her *Englisch* friend that she was newly married. Immediately, Truda informed her that the Word of God was the best marriage manual known to man. She encouraged Sarah to read chapter thirteen of First Corinthians. First Corinthians Thirteen spoke of charity, which she learned meant 'love in action'. All the good works in the world didn't matter, if one did not possess charity.

What a clear picture she'd been given when Saul kissed her.

Oh, the day when he'd hold her in his arms and it would actually mean something! Had he kissed her out of pity? Or had it been penance for the guilt he was feeling? Was he even thinking of her, or did he imagine Chloe, when their lips met? Sarah sighed. Would Saul ever be able to get over his lost love and learn to love another?

FOUR

*S*alome Brenneman anxiously waited in the buggy while her husband hitched up the gelding. If he didn't hurry, they'd arrive late and she couldn't bear the thought of adding any more stress to poor Sarah's life. She was confident that her son would eventually make a good husband someday, but as far as she knew, he hadn't attempted any accolades. In fact, it didn't even seem as though he cared for the young woman.

Well, whether Saul loved the girl or not, Salome was determined to welcome her into the family with open arms. After all, Sarah was carrying their *grossboppli*. To admit the truth, Salome felt somewhat responsible, as though she had a part in the pregnancy. If she and Eb had kept tighter reins on their *kinner*, would this have happened? Of course, she couldn't know for sure.

Nevertheless, she couldn't help but question the wisdom of their ways now. Was it wise to let young couples go off alone at night for hours on end? It just went to prove that open-top buggies were not enough safeguard against the temptations of sin. She was ever so thankful that their district didn't practice bed courtship. She couldn't imagine the unexpected pregnancies that occurred in the Old Order districts that still practiced the old custom. *Eb certainly wouldn't have kept his hands to himself,* she chuckled at the thought.

"What's so funny?" Eb smiled and slid into the driver's side of the bench seat.

"*Ach,* it's nothin'. Just rememberin' our courtin' days, that's all."

"Oh? I don't remember anything funny about our courtin' days."

"Of course not. You were too busy tryin' to steal kisses from me, remember?"

Eb's eyes sparkled with mirth. "Oh, I remember." He provoked his wife by slowly moving his hand up her leg.

"*Ach,* Ebenezer Brenneman! You should be ashamed of yourself, behaving unseemly in broad daylight."

Eb chortled at her disconcerted expression. He always loved getting a rise out of his *fraa.* "Now, you know I don't like it when you call me by my full name. I think you owe me a kiss for that." He leaned over and kissed his wife on the lips before she had a chance to protest. "There. Now I'm ready to go."

Salome shook her head. *No wonder Saul's in this predicament; he's just like his father! I guess the apple doesn't fall far from the tree.*

Sarah removed the handkerchief from inside her sleeve and wiped the sweat from her brow as she waited for the kitchen timer to sound. Today had been one of the most hectic days of her life and she dreaded the prospect of company. What she felt like doing was crashing on her bed and taking a long nap. Her feet ached from being on them all day. She usually had extra time during the day to take small breaks every now and then, but there was no time for it today.

Fortunately, Saul had been pleasant this morning. She guessed that he was excited about his folks coming to visit since he mentioned the fact three times before heading off to work for the day. Sarah realized he was due home in a few minutes when she glanced up at the wall clock. She hoped he was in a good mood because she didn't know if she could deal with any more stress.

Sarah opened the pantry and pulled out a clean rag to wipe down the counters again. She wanted to make a good impression on Saul's folks, because she was certain they couldn't think good of her after what she and Saul had done. She suspected most people in the community looked on her with contempt; it was just human nature, she supposed. At least Saul agreed to marry her, albeit lamentably. She couldn't imagine how much more difficult things would be if she had to bring a *boppli* into the world alone.

A buzzing sound drew her attention back to the oven and she pulled out the chicken pot pie. The delicious aroma filled the air and she laughed when her stomach growled in response. She glanced at the place settings on the table to make sure she hadn't forgotten anything, when Saul walked through the door.

"Mmm...somethin' smells *appeditlich*." He took an exaggerated whiff, then set his insulated lunch container on the counter.

"*Ach*, Saul. I just cleaned that counter for the third time today. Could you just put your lunch box in the pantry? I don't have time to clean it out right now," she requested.

Saul walked back over to his lunch box and whisked it off the counter. "No problem." He glanced around the kitchen. "Do you need help with anything?"

"*Nee*. Just go take your shower before your folks arrive," she insisted.

Instead of obeying her directive, Sarah felt Saul standing directly behind her. The smell of sawdust and hard work lingered on his clothing. His closeness frustrated her to no end. She desired Saul's attention, but she knew it wasn't sincere. His hot breath on her neck flustered her further. If he didn't stop doing this, she knew she'd eventually succumb to temptation.

"Your shower?" she squeaked out.

Saul straightened and cleared his throat. "As you wish, *fraa*."

A sigh of relief escaped Sarah's lips when she heard Saul's footsteps moving in the opposite direction and the click of the closing bathroom door. Good, now she could concentrate on the task at hand: dessert. She hoped Saul's folks liked chocolate Shoofly Pie.

Sarah surveyed the table once again, satisfied that everything was now in order and ready for company. She glanced down at her dirty apron and noticed she'd soiled her sleeve with molasses while making the Shoofly Pie. Well, almost everything was ready. She peeked out the window to make sure Saul's folks hadn't arrived, then quickly headed to the bedroom to change.

Unlike himself of late, Saul had actually been in a good mood all day. He found that when he refocused his thoughts, life didn't seem all that bad. Thoughts of Chloe still filled his mind daily, but he attempted to suppress them. He noticed that contemplations of her only brought him despair.

And he remembered Sarah.

The pained look on her face when he'd kissed her. She knew she was second place in his heart and so did he. But what could he do? He knew his love for Chloe would never die.

Saul sighed. He didn't have time to be pondering these things when his parents were on the brink of arriving. He stepped out of the shower and hastily grabbed a towel. After a quick glance around, he realized he'd forgotten his clothes. Fortunately, Sarah was still in the kitchen. He could make a dash to the bedroom and she probably wouldn't even notice. He wrapped the towel around his waist and hastened to his room, or Sarah's, more accurately.

Saul whisked the door open, only to be greeted with a gasp. He looked up to see his wife in her undergarments and his face immediately felt like it was on fire.

"*Ach*, Saul. What are you doin'?" Sarah quickly crossed her arms over her bosom to hide herself.

"I…uh…forgot my clothes." He knew he should look away, but he couldn't take his eyes off her. She was breathtaking, even with her rounded belly – especially with her round belly. He stood gawking at his *fraa* for a few seconds, then felt as though a magnet were pulling him toward her. He forgot about his clothes and the reason for coming into the room. He forgot that his folks would be arriving shortly and they would be enjoying a meal together. Nothing, other than his wife standing before him, could penetrate his thoughts at this moment. Not even Chloe.

Saul now stood mesmerized in front of Sarah and caressed a lock of hair that trailed down her arm. Sarah stood silent and still, her breaths short and shallow, as though she were a deer caught in the headlights. Saul bent down and kissed her neck.

Sarah swallowed. "Saul? Your folks…" Her voice stopped when his lips found hers.

"Hello-o?"

A whispered curse escaped Saul's lips as he heard his mother's voice ring through the *dawdi haus*. He grudgingly released Sarah from his embrace, realizing they both had yet to don their clothing. He was tempted to forego supper and tell his parents to come back another day. Saul cleared his throat and quickly went to the bedroom door. "We'll be out in just a minute, *Mamm*."

A look of relief flooded Sarah's countenance. "*Ach*, we still need to get dressed." She quickly turned toward the closet and shuffled through her dresses, choosing a purple one for the occasion. She felt Saul's presence behind her, reticent to turn around. Sensing he needed to say something, Sarah waited patiently.

"Sarah...*jah*, you're right. We should get dressed." He moved to the dresser on the opposite side of the room, pulled out his boxers and a t-shirt, and hastily slipped them on. When he moved back to the closet, Sarah already had her dress on and was pinning her apron in place. He watched as she slipped from the room to greet his parents. Saul released a groan of frustration.

The necessity to compose herself before seeing Saul's folks propelled Sarah to the restroom. She turned on the sink and quickly splashed cool water on her burning face. *Why did I let him do that?* Sarah chided herself for being so vulnerable.

She'd told Saul she didn't want his body without his soul and she meant it. But it seemed her own heart and mind were not in agreement. Seeing Saul wrapped in a towel without his shirt on stirred desire in her heart. And when he approached her and took her into his arms, she felt like she couldn't move, as though she were helpless to do anything but acquiesce. She didn't *want* to say no. *Lord, I'm in trouble. Please help me stay my course. Help me not to settle for less than my husband's love.*

FIVE

*S*alome watched as Sarah and Saul eventually made their way into the kitchen. She couldn't get over the feeling that maybe she and Eb had interrupted something. Perhaps she should have let Eb take his time hitching up the carriage. Maybe Saul's marriage didn't need as much help as she thought it did.

"*Denki* for coming, Salome. I hope you and Eb like chicken pot pie," Sarah said, bringing the main dish to the table. She'd had it warming on the stove and now the aroma filled the whole house.

Eb's eyebrows shot up. "Chicken pot pie is one my favorite dishes. Did Saul tell you that?"

Saul cast a look at Sarah and Salome didn't miss the added color in her cheeks. Yep, they definitely interrupted something.

"Uh, no," Sarah said. "I just guessed. I think most folks like chicken pot pie, jah?"

"Shall we sit down for supper?" Saul suggested, offering his father the head chair.

"No, *sohn*. This is your household. You get the honor. I'll take the chair at the other end," Eb said. Of course, with only four chairs at the small table, there weren't many options.

Saul nodded and bowed his head in silent prayer.

Saul thought of his father's words and let the idea rattle around in his head. *I am the head of this household. I am responsible for Sarah and the* boppli *she carries. It is an honor to be the head of the house.* Saul never viewed his role as an honor; instead it had seemed like more of a curse to him. At seventeen, it seemed like an overwhelming responsibility.

Saul lifted his eyes to Sarah, remembering their brief time in the bedroom. *Yes, being a husband was an honor.* His lips curved up in a smile. Suddenly, he couldn't wait till his folks left for the night.

"Mm...this chicken pot pie is *gut*, Sarah," Salome commented. She wanted to be an encouragement to her new daughter-in-law, so she wouldn't mention the fact that she could tell she'd used canned chicken.

"It doesn't taste as *gut* as yours, *Mamm*," Saul said, shoving another forkful in his mouth. "But I guess it's all right."

Salome noticed tears spring to Sarah's eyes. Had she not taught her son to be more considerate? "*Ach*, Saul." She shook her head in disapproval, alerting Saul to his hurtful words.

Saul glanced at his wife, whose head was down. "What did I say?"

Sarah abruptly arose from the table and hurried to the restroom, to Saul's dismay.

"Saul, I thought I taught you that if you don't have something encouraging to say then it's best not to say anything," his mother chided.

"What did I say, *Mamm*?"

Was her son really that dense? She couldn't help the uncharitable thought. Her eyes pleaded with Eb's for help. Saul could be exasperating.

"Come on, *sohn*. Let's go outside for a bit," Eb suggested, wiping his mouth with a paper towel.

Saul shook his head, but followed his father outside nevertheless.

Saul paced the small porch on the back of the *dawdi haus*. "I don't understand her, *Dat*. It seems like Sarah cries about every little thing. Why would she cry about something as *dumm* as that?"

"You don't need to understand her, *sohn*. You just need to understand how to behave around her. Women are sensitive

– especially when they're in the family way. To her it is not *dumm*. She has been working hard all day to prepare supper and to make sure the house is nice for your folks. Don't you think it makes her feel bad that you only have discouraging words to say? And in front of your folks nonetheless."

Saul shrugged. "I guess so." He scratched his head. "Say, *Dat*? What do you think of...well, you know...the marriage bed? I mean, I kissed *mei fraa* the other night and she refused me. She said she didn't want my body without my soul. Whatever that meant."

Eb had to hold in a chuckle. *Just like a man.* "You have to learn to love your *fraa*. You want her, right?"

An image of Sarah in her undergarments flashed through his mind. He smiled sheepishly. "*Jah.*"

"And you think you *should* have her because she's your wife, no? It is her duty to meet your needs."

"Well, *jah.*"

"Take a look at your motives, Saul. Are you not being selfish? Are you considering her wishes and her needs? Love is not self-seeking. Remember that Christ was our example. He came to serve, not to be served. He gave of himself fully, not considering his own needs."

"But I could never be that."

"You don't need to be perfect, but you do need to make an effort. Sarah will notice."

Salome knocked on the bathroom door and waited for Sarah to emerge. Her daughter-in-law's eyes were puffy and she sympathized with her. She'd been through her own share of inconsiderate remarks when she and Eb were newly married.

"*Ach*, I'm sorry," Sarah apologized, dabbing at her eyes again. "It must be this *boppli*. I'm usually not such a cry baby."

"No, don't apologize. What Saul said hurt. I'm sorry that you had to be at the brunt of my son's insensitivity. You two are so young and I'm afraid Saul still has a lot of maturing to do. And things do seem to impact a woman more when she is in the family way." Salome grinned at Sarah, hoping to coax a smile. "You know, it's kind of funny. Saul has no idea what he said to offend you."

"*Jah*, I guess that is kind of funny." Sarah giggled, thinking of Saul's clueless expression. "*Denki*, Salome, for your kindness."

"Sarah, I hope you and I can become *gut* friends. And I want you to know that you can come to me for anything."

Sarah nodded in appreciation.

After Saul's mother had shooed both him and Sarah out of the kitchen, insisting that Sarah put her feet up and relax, they now sat alone in the small living room together.

"My folks think that I should apologize for what I said earlier," Saul said. "I guess I said the wrong thing."

"And what do you think, Saul?" Sarah seemed a little put out by him.

He shrugged. "I reckon if I said something to offend you, I should apologize."

"Saul, you're not a child anymore. Your folks shouldn't have to tell you to apologize. I don't want an apology that doesn't mean anything," she said emphatically.

Exasperated, Saul rose from the couch. "Fine. I won't apologize. I don't think I did anything wrong anyway. A person has a right to state their honest opinion, and that was my honest opinion. If you can't deal with it, then I don't know what to say to you!" Saul needed to leave before he said anything else that 'offended' her. *Ugh, this woman is so frustrating.* He stomped out of the living room and plopped himself down at the dining room table.

Eb walked in from the kitchen and noticed Saul at the table with his head in his hands. "What's going on, *sohn*? Why aren't you in there with your *fraa*?"

"*Dat*, I don't understand her. I was going to apologize just like you said, but she said she didn't want me to. She said I'm not sincere." He huffed.

"Well, are you?"

"I didn't do anything wrong, *Dat*. I was just stating my honest opinion."

"Let me ask you a question, *sohn*. If it were *Chloe* you offended instead of Sarah –"

"I would never do anything to hurt Chloe. And don't bring her up, it's not the same thing."

"Like I was saying – please show your *vadder* enough respect to listen," Eb reprimanded. "*If* it were Chloe you offended, would you have trouble apologizing?"

"That's not fair, *Dat*."

"And you think you're being fair to your *fraa*? Imagine how she feels always being compared to Chloe. Sarah knows she'll never measure up in your mind." Eb squeezed his son's shoulder. "You need to let your former *aldi* go. You must give her up in every part of your life, including your thoughts. Move on with your life, Saul. Sarah is carrying your *boppli*. That should mean something to you."

Saul pondered his father's words, then sighed in surrender. "You're right, Daed," he acknowledged.

"Let's go back in and join the ladies, shall we?"

"Oh good, you two are done with your little chat," Salome said.

Saul glanced around the small living room and took a seat on one of the hickory rockers.

"I sent Sarah into the bedroom to rest. Poor girl is plain worn out." She studied her son. "You should be helping her out more. Being in the family way takes a lot out of a *maedel*."

"Got it, *Mamm*," Saul said, releasing a sigh.

Sarah emerged from the bedroom. "I'll get dessert ready now."

"Saul, you help her," his mother suggested.

Saul obeyed his *mamm's* request and followed his wife into the kitchen.

Salome and Eb watched as the young couple disappeared into the other room, then Salome quickly signaled her husband near. "Look at that," she whispered, pointing to a folded blanket under the small end table. "I bet Saul's been sleeping out here on the sofa. No wonder those two are having so much trouble. I know how grumpy you get when we don't—"

"Salome, what are you up to?" Eb's eyebrows arched.

"Don't you worry, *lieb*. Just play along." Salome patted Eb's hand.

Saul stepped into the *schtupp* and invited his parents into the dining area to enjoy some Shoofly Pie.

"Oh!"

Saul's eyes widened as his mother moaned. Sarah came rushing in to the room as well.

Salome's hand went to her forehead and she closed her eyes. "I'm coming down with an agonizing headache. Eb, you'll have to go eat some of that wonderful dessert without me. In fact, if I don't feel better soon, you'll need to go home by yourself." Salome completely overdramatized her nonexistent pain. But how else was she to get Saul and Sarah to work out their differences?

Eb's jaw fell open. "Ah, Salome. I'd hate to do that," he protested.

"You know how all that jostling in the buggy just makes my headaches worse," she reminded him, then turned to Saul and Sarah. "And don't you two worry. I can sleep right here on the couch."

Sarah pasted on a clearly fake smile and helplessly looked at Saul. He raised his eyebrows and shrugged, a smirk forming near the tip of his mouth.

SIX

*S*arah turned toward the wall and nervously unpinned her apron. The door closing behind Saul indicated he'd completed his nightly routine and entered the bedroom. Sarah thought Saul's mother's sudden headache seemed a bit strange, but she wasn't about to accuse the woman of pretending, if that was indeed what she was doing.

It was clear to Sarah that Saul's parents loved them and apparently would do just about anything to see them happy. That she was thankful for. At least the *boppli* would have grandparents that cared. She truly enjoyed Eb and Salome's company.

Why couldn't Saul be more like his folks? If he could just learn to be civil, they might make it a whole day without arguing.

"Sarah?" Saul's voice spoke from behind her.

She nodded, unfastening the pin that held her *kapp* to her hair. She removed her *kapp* and pulled the cape of her apron over her head.

"I'm sorry for earlier."

"What are you sorry for, Saul?" Was he simply apologizing to get into her good graces?

"I know that what I said offended you. I didn't intend to hurt you." He tentatively placed his hand on her shoulder. "Will you forgive me?" He nearly whispered the words in her ear.

Sarah took a step away. It was difficult to concentrate with him standing so close. "*Jah*, Saul, I'll forgive you."

He released a breath. "*Gut.*" He stepped closer to his wife and watched as she removed the pins from her waist apron. "Let me help with that."

Sarah allowed Saul to 'help' her, although she was perfectly capable of getting undressed by herself. What could she say to Saul to make him understand that she wasn't ready for a physical relationship? She thought she'd been clear the other day, but he didn't seem to get it.

Saul reached under Sarah's chin to unfasten her dress.

This has to stop. "Saul, don't you need to change?" She thought redirecting his attention elsewhere might provide a chance for her to change into her nightdress quickly, before he could offer any more assistance.

"*Nee.* I want to help my *fraa.*" His blue eyes glowed and Sarah was having a difficult time resisting him. This would be a much easier task if her husband wasn't so irresistibly attractive.

"Saul, I–"

His kisses once again cut off her speech and she wondered if this would become a game he often played when he didn't want her to continue. Was he deliberately halting her words?

Sarah forced herself away. "No, Saul."

His blue eyes studied her intently. "What do you mean, 'no'? You're my wife. I know you want it too. I see it in your eyes. I can feel it in your kiss."

Saul was absolutely correct. She did want him. She wanted him more than just about anything. But she had to fight that desire. They'd already made too many mistakes. She couldn't bear to make another one. "No, not like this. I want your love. I know you don't love me."

He didn't deny it. "What does it matter? We're married, Sarah."

"It matters to *me*. Please, Saul. We're not ready for this yet."

Saul chuckled and placed his hand on her expanded belly. "Not ready? Well, it appears to be a little late for that. We have a *boppli* right here and last I heard, we got hitched."

"That's true but–"

"There are no buts, Sarah. We are one now. You belong to me." He continued to unfasten her dress.

She did not desire an argument, but it seemed there was no choice. *Why can't he understand that I don't want to do this?* Perhaps she needed to be more direct. "Saul, I don't want to do this." She stepped out of his reach.

"Are you denying me my rights as your husband? I have needs, Sarah. I know you don't want me to get my needs met elsewhere, do you?"

Tears flooded her eyes. "That's not fair, Saul!"

"Do you think any of this is fair?"

"I have needs too! I'm a *person*, Saul. I'm not an object. Will you please, for once, think of someone other than yourself?"

"For once? You've got to be kidding! I *married* you, Sarah. I left someone I *loved* and I married you. You could have gone somewhere and given the *boppli* up. There's a whole lot more people in the world that want a baby more than I do."

Sarah stood speechless. How could anyone say such hurtful words? She moved past Saul to the dresser and with shaky hands, pulled out her nightgown. There was no way she was going to stay here in this room with this man. Sarah ran out of the room and slipped out the side door of the house, not wanting to awaken Saul's mother. She didn't know how his *mamm* could possibly sleep through all their arguing.

"Argh!" Saul kicked the side of the bed in frustration and now his toe throbbed. *Why does that woman have to be so difficult?* He slipped off his suspenders, hastily removed his clothing, threw them in the corner, and plopped onto bed. Alone.

Saul took a deep breath and stared up at the ceiling. Oh, how he wished he could close his eyes and make this whole nightmare go away! *Why does life have to be so hard, God? Why couldn't you have just let Chloe and I stay together? She wasn't like this, Lord.* He closed his eyes and waited for sleep to come, but it would not. Instead, negative thoughts relentlessly assaulted his psyche.

Saul punched his pillow and turned over on his other side again. An hour passed…then two. Still Saul couldn't fall asleep. Feelings of guilt now inundated his consciousness. Perhaps he shouldn't have said those things to Sarah. After all, she was pretty much stuck with him too. It never occurred to him that maybe *she'd* had other plans for her life as well. She was right. He was being selfish.

Hadn't his *vadder* said the same thing? He'd been right about a lot of things. He said if Saul didn't give Chloe up, he and Sarah would never have a stable relationship. But he couldn't bear the thought of letting Chloe go forever. *But I've already lost her. I'll never get her back.* Saul heaved a sigh of defeat.

He sat up in the bed and retrieved his wallet from the nightstand. Grudgingly, he opened it up and pulled out the photo strip from Ocean City. He gazed upon it one last time, cherishing the memory, then with a heavy heart, Saul dropped the photos into the waste basket near the door. *Goodbye, Chloe.*

It was over now. Completely over.

Saul grieved momentarily, then his father's words came back to him, "If you're always looking back at what you've lost, you'll never discover the treasure that lies just up ahead."

Do you have treasure up ahead for Sarah and me, Lord? It was certainly difficult to comprehend.

All he knew was that he wasn't going to accomplish anything unless he smoothed things over with his *fraa*. Retrieving his pants from the corner, he said a prayer. Hopefully, he could converse with his wife in a civil manner without blowing his top. And just maybe he could convince her to come home.

Bishop Mast nudged his wife. "Did you hear that?"

She rolled over and pried her sleepy eyelids open. This was the second time she'd been awakened from a deep sleep this evening and now the unwanted impositions were beginning to become bothersome. As the bishop's wife, she'd become some-what accustomed over the years to interferences in their sched-ule. But it was the nightly intrusions that were the worst. "What is it now?"

"Sounds like someone's knocking on the door."

"Well, do you want *me* to get it?"

"No, no." He huffed and rolled out of bed. "I'll get it."

The bishop hastily threw his clothes on and hurried toward the door. Fortunately, all the children's rooms were upstairs and they wouldn't hear the knocking. He didn't have to guess who might be standing outside the door. He pulled the door open.

"What do you need, Saul?" he asked brusquely. He wasn't exactly thrilled that his new son-in-law wasn't treating his daughter well.

"I want to talk to Sarah."

"She's sleeping. Come back in the morning." Bishop Mast began closing the door.

"Wait, *Dat*," Sarah spoke from behind him.

"I didn't realize you were awake, *dochder*. Are you sure you want to speak with him?"

His downhearted daughter shrugged.

"Please?" Saul spoke up, requesting an audience with his wife.

Bishop Mast nodded. "Very well, then. I'm going back to bed and don't intend to be woken up again until chorin' time. Is that understood?" He eyed the young couple wearily.

They both nodded sheepishly as though they were two young children receiving a scolding.

Saul and Sarah stood near the back door in the Masts' kitchen. Saul looked into his wife's puffy eyes and guilt once again pricked his heart. What could he say to convince her to come home with him? Would she allow him to touch her? He opened his arms and waited until Sarah filled them with her presence. Saul wrapped his arms around his wife and held her for several minutes in silence.

"You were right, Sarah. I was being selfish," he spoke the words into her hair.

His confession produced a subdued sob.

"I'm sorry for saying the things I said. Will you forgive me for being such a *dummkopp*?"

Sarah let out a tiny giggle.

Saul pulled back and made a funny face. "I hope that was a yes." He smiled.

Sarah smiled back and nodded.

"*Gut*," – Saul bent down and lifted Sarah off the ground – "because I'm dying to take you to bed." His eyes glistened with mischief.

Sarah gasped and sent a warning. "Sa-ul…"

"I'm really tired," he explained, then exaggerated a yawn.

Sarah quickly realized he'd been teasing her and smiled.

Early morning sunlight streamed through the crack between the dark shade and the window frame. Sarah's eyes slowly flitted open, although she wasn't sure she wanted to awaken from her peaceful sleep. A smile played on her lips as she found herself nestled against her husband's chest, his strong arm draped around her.

They had agreed not to touch each other and keep to their own sides of the bed, but apparently they must've somehow found each other during the night. They'd lain awake talking an extra hour after returning from Sarah's folks' place and Saul had been a perfect gentleman.

The smell of bacon now wafted through the air and Sarah suspected Saul's mother had begun preparing breakfast. She knew she should get up and help, but hesitated to leave the contentment of lying in Saul's arms next to his warm body.

Sarah felt Saul move and glanced up at his handsome face. *Ach*, was he really her husband? The dark hair on his face, that seemed to fill in by the day, indicated it was so. Saul's eyes opened and he smiled down at her.

"*Guten mayrie, fraa.*" He pressed his lips to the top of her head.

Sarah smiled back at him. "I think your *mamm* is fixin' breakfast." Sarah began to rise, but Saul halted her.

"*Nee*, just lay here in my arms a few more minutes."

Sarah thought of pinching herself to see whether she was dreaming. She had to admit to herself that she was quickly falling in love with this man by her side. When Saul arrived at her folks place early this morning, a glimmer of hope filtered through the ominous clouds surrounding her heart.

Although she'd been truly exasperated with her insensitive husband, she prayed that God would somehow make this fragile relationship work. She admitted that neither one of them knew what they were doing, nor had they been ready for these struggles. Only with help from *Der Herr* would they be able to survive. Perhaps He could knit their hearts together as only the God of love can.

After the sound of Salome setting the table reached their ears, she figured they'd better get dressed for the day. Truth be known, she'd be content to lie next to Saul all day long listening to the steady beat of his heart. But what respectable Amish woman would stay in bed all day?

"We should get up now, *jah*?"

"If that's what you'd like, *fraa*."

"*Nee*, it's what we need to do." Sarah sat up and swung her feet over the side of the bed. "You've got to be to work in just a little bit. I'm certain you'll want breakfast too."

"You're right. It must be about seven now, *jah*? We've practically spent the whole day in bed." Saul grinned.

His jovial tone caught Sarah off-guard. Saul was much easier to love when he spoke cheerfully.

Sarah smiled. "*Ach*, did your folks say that too?"

"I wouldn't know. I've never slept past five." Saul's eyes sparkled.

Sarah picked up her pillow and tossed it at him.

"Ah, you wanna fight, huh?" He picked up his own pillow and thwacked her across the back.

She picked it up, intercepting her own pillow that he'd catapulted, and smacked him across the face.

Saul chuckled. "So, you wanna play dirty? Come here, *fraa*." He hopped over the bed, but Sarah ran around to the other side, giggling.

Saul swiftly followed her around the bed.

She attempted to climb over, but she didn't make it. Saul barely clasped her ankle before she made it over to the other side. He pulled her feet toward him, causing her to turn on her back, until she lay directly in front of him. He then reached his hands out and began tickling her sides relentlessly. She'd never laughed so much in her life.

Sarah was nearly out of breath when Saul bent down to kiss her. Delighting in his attention, she instinctively pulled him down next to her. Her heart beat rapidly, but she had no desire to tell Saul to stop. His kisses felt so right. She forgot about the time of day and goings on around them. The only thing that mattered was here and now – the love between a husband and wife.

That is, until Salome knocked on the door announcing breakfast was ready and on the table.

Sarah looked up at Saul with a look of frustration, then they both simultaneously burst into laughter.

"We'll be out in just a minute, *Mamm*," Saul called out.

SEVEN

*S*arah ran her fingers over her lips once again, remembering Saul's delicious kisses from several hours before when he'd bid her farewell for the day. She couldn't wait until he returned this evening. She'd queried Salome about Saul's favorite dish, before Saul had taken his mother home, and it was baking in the oven at this very moment. She should've guessed what it was.

Now, she needed to do some quick cleaning up. She'd made the bed this morning, but she'd been in a hurry because of their waiting breakfast. Now that she had more time, she'd be able to do the job properly like *Mamm* had taught her growing up. *Mamm* had said, "It's okay to give somethin' a lick and a promise. But just be sure you keep your promises."

She entered the bedroom with a dusting rag in hand. If this was her and Saul's private abode, she wanted it to be as special as possible. She dusted the small nightstand and the larger bureau, taking particular care not to knock over the oil lamp that sat in the middle. Sometimes she didn't mind being Amish so much. Like now, when she didn't have hordes of knickknacks to dust like some *Englischers* did.

Sarah went to her top dresser drawer and pulled out some sweet pea perfume she'd purchased at the mall as a special treat. She misted the sheets with a few sprays of the delightful fragrance and the lovely scent floated through the air. She wondered if Saul would like it or if he'd think she was silly.

Oh, the change in Saul! When Sarah had prayed the night before, she didn't expect the answer to come so quickly. It seemed as though Saul was a brand new man. Of course, only time would tell for sure and for certain.

After the bed was made, Sarah picked up the trash can to empty it out. Taking one more look around the room, satisfied that it was in shipshape order, she waltzed out.

The smell of supper, when she entered the kitchen, made her smile. What would Saul's reaction be? She hoped he'd be pleased. If the survival of their marriage depended on her, she was going to do everything in her power to make it work. She knew now that she loved Saul, and she wasn't about to lose him to anyone.

When Sarah dumped the small wastebasket from their bedroom into the large kitchen trashcan, something caught her eye. *What are these doing here?* Sarah's heart sank, yet the moment was bittersweet. She lifted out Saul's photo strip of him and Chloe, wiped off the coffee grounds they'd fallen into, and tucked them in her apron pocket. *This meant so much to him.*

She quickly went to the bedroom, opened up her dower chest, and put them away for safe keeping.

Thinking about Saul giving up the photos, and how much they'd meant to him, made Sarah's heart soar. *Does that mean he loves me? What else could it mean?* One thing she knew for sure and for certain, Saul giving up those photos meant more than any words ever could. She realized how painful it must've been for him and appreciated Saul all the more.

Sarah smiled with renewed confidence. *This marriage is going to work out after all.* Denki, Vadder.

The sound of carriage wheels drew her attention to the barn and butterflies filled her stomach. She quickly set the table, making sure everything was just so.

Saul whistled as he strode toward the steps of the small *dawdi haus*. Most of the day his thoughts had been inundated with his *fraa* and the time they'd shared talking last night. And, of course, he hadn't forgotten the fun they'd indulged in this morning either. It had felt so good to play like one of the *kinner* again. Saul realized he hadn't felt this lighthearted in a long time. It seemed all the stress of finding out about Sarah's predicament, and his consequential break up with Chloe, had stolen his happiness and he was glad to finally gain it back. He had been walking through a fog, but now that the haze had begun to lift, he was seeing more clearly than ever.

Sarah wasn't at all how Saul assumed she'd be. Because of her father, the bishop of their district, and how strict he was known to be, he'd misjudged her. For some reason he expected her to be dull and boring, but he discovered his *fraa* wasn't that at all. He looked forward to the days ahead and getting to know her better.

He had to watch himself, he realized, because he almost got carried away with Sarah this morning. Thankfully his mother intervened when informing them that breakfast was ready. The last thing he wanted is for his wife to feel that he'd taken advantage of her, and that meant stepping lightly in the passion department.

Sarah had said that she wanted all of him, but the truth was, he wasn't all there yet. He knew Chloe would always have a special place in his heart. How could someone just forget one they'd loved so deeply? Although he'd thrown the photos away, he didn't know how to go about forgetting Chloe. When certain things happened throughout the day, she seemed to pop into his mind unbidden, stealing his thoughts. But he realized now he had no business thinking about Chloe when he was married to another woman – a wonderful woman at that. Sarah deserved his best. He determined to let the past lie and move on.

So he devised a plan that he believed Sarah would enjoy.

Saul opened the door to be greeted with the most delicious aroma he'd ever smelled: homemade macaroni and cheese! His shining eyes moved to Sarah's and she graced him with a beautiful smile. How her countenance glowed this evening! Everything about her seemed to radiate joy and for the first time, Saul felt like the husband he should be – the one he should have been all along.

He dropped his lunch box near the sink and drew his wife into his arms. "Have I ever told you that I love you?" Saul felt a small gasp escape Sarah's lips – apparently she hadn't expected to hear it – but she smiled nonetheless.

"No, I don't believe you have, husband." Her eyes twinkled as Saul bent down and kissed her.

"I love you, Sarah," he uttered, then kissed his wife again. "I love you, *fraa*." Another kiss. "*Ich liebe dich, schatzi.*"

Sarah giggled when the stubble from his beard tickled her neck. "What are you doing, silly?"

"I'm making up for lost time." He smiled and kissed her again.

"But supper…" She gasped.

Saul reluctantly released her. "You're right. We should eat the delicious meal you've prepared." He moved to his seat at the head of the small table and sat down. Sarah set the food on the table and quickly joined him. "And afterwards, if you're feeling up to it, I'd like to take you somewhere."

Sarah's eyebrows rose. "Oh? And where's that?"

"Patience, *mei fraa*, you'll have to wait and see." Saul winked, delighting in his successful evening thus far.

Sarah opened the lid to the dish on the table and Saul's face brightened even more.

"Is that what I think it is?"

Sarah tapped her finger on her chin. "Hmm...depends on what you think it is."

"Mac 'n cheese?"

Sarah nodded.

"This day just keeps on getting better." He smiled and reached for her hand across the table. They both bowed their heads and gave a silent thanks for their numerous blessings.

Saul rubbed the back of his neck and discreetly glanced over at Sarah sitting in the seat next to him. Her contentment helped him relax some, but in truth, he was nervous. This was officially their first date as a wedded couple, which seemed comical to Saul. Or it would be if he could stop his hands from sweating. The last time he felt like this was when he went to meet Chloe's folks after they'd forbidden her to see him unsupervised.

No, you are not going to think about Chloe! He reprimanded himself in frustration.

He reached over and grasped his wife's hand and she scooted a little closer. It would be difficult to keep the promise he'd made to himself.

Saul brought the buggy to a stop, making certain he was off the main road a ways. He hopped down from the buggy and beckoned Sarah to join him, offering his hand for assistance in descending the carriage.

Sarah looked around and lowered her eyebrows. "We're at the bridge."

Saul nodded, but kept silent. It was fun to keep his *fraa* guessing. He and Sarah walked to the bridge hand in hand.

"It's closed." Sarah frowned.

"*Jah*, it's a private bridge now. I guess they don't want it getting' messed up."

"But what's the point in keepin' it closed? Nobody can enjoy it now."

"Sure we can. Come." Saul led her to the rock wall near the bridge's entrance. "You know they call 'em kissin' bridges, right?"

Sarah nodded. A smidgen of pink blossomed on her cheeks.

"Well, I aim to take my *fraa* to all, or mostly all at least, of the bridges in Lancaster County." His eyes gleamed with mischief from under his black hat brim. "And *buss*."

Sarah gasped. "You want to kiss under every bridge in Lancaster County?"

Saul nodded and drew Sarah close. "Starting right now," he whispered huskily into her ear.

"But we're out in the open. What if someone sees?"

"I don't think your *vadder* followed us, do you? I'm certain sure no one is going to complain about a man kissin' his *fraa*. Besides," he pulled her to the side of the bridge out of direct view of the traffic, "nobody will see us here."

When Saul noticed the concern fade from her eyes, he drew her near and gently pressed his lips to hers. His senses piqued with delight as she pulled him closer and fervently engaged in the kiss. He never expected to find this much pleasure with Sarah as his wife, but somehow *Der Herr* seemed to be guiding their footsteps now.

Saul reluctantly, but necessarily, forced himself away.

When Sarah caught her breath, Saul realized she'd enjoyed the kiss as much as he had – which he didn't think possible.

"I think I like your plan, but how will we get back before dark if we go to the bridges out yonder?"

Saul's eyes twinkled again. "I've already figured that out. We can either do one of two things: leave early on a Saturday and make a day of it, or we can stay at a motel for the night."

"*Ach*, really, Saul?" She positively glowed.

Saul thought she might reject the mention of staying over-night, but instead she beamed with excitement. "You would like that?"

Sarah bit her bottom lip and pulled him close once more. "*Jah*, Saul. I would like it very much," she whispered, before offering another toe-curling kiss.

EIGHT

*T*o say that God had breathed new life into their marriage would have been absolutely correct, Sarah pondered. The last couple of months felt like a mixture of pure bliss combined with torment. Every day it seemed she grew closer to *Der Herr* while reading His Word. And as much as she loved Saul, she cherished the time when he would leave for the day and she could read her *verboten* English Bible. She hadn't shared it with Saul, for fear he'd be upset. Nor had she told him of her secret meetings with her friend Truda.

Today she and Truda would be meeting again. Nothing excited Sarah more than learning about *Der Herr* and His gracious love. She yearned to share her newfound truths with Saul, but to do so could prove disastrous for their marriage. That fact unsettled her to no end. There had been others that had gone down a similar path and it *always* resulted in heartache.

As soon as she'd made sure the house was in order, she headed toward the barn to hitch up the driving horse. Like many Amish families, they owned two horses. Since Saul had taken the open top buggy, she would take the enclosed one, which she preferred anyway. The sound of hoof beats approaching caused Sarah to pause at the barn door.

Saul.

What is he doing home right now? It was only eleven o'clock. Hopefully nothing was wrong.

Saul brought the horse and carriage to a stop just short of where Sarah stood. "Sarah?" Saul's brow lowered. "What are you doing out here?" He glanced down at the purse on her forearm. "Are you planning to go somewhere?"

Sarah swallowed. *Oh no, how can I explain this to him?* "Uh, *jah.* I was just going to town." She glanced away briefly. "You're home. Is everything okay?"

"*Jah,* it's *wunderbaar.* I thought I'd surprise my beautiful *fraa* and treat her to dinner today." His eyes shone until he noticed her frown. "You don't want to go?"

Sarah cringed inside when she detected disappointment in his gaze. "No, I mean, *jah.* I do want to have dinner with you. It's just that I…" She took a deep breath, attempting to gather her frantic thoughts. "I planned to meet somebody."

"That's perfect. We can ride together. I needed to go by the hardware store. *Dat* and I are running low on a few things." Saul jumped down from the buggy to help her in. It seemed like she needed more assistance with everything lately. She felt like a wobbling duck with her belly growing so rapidly.

Sarah stared out at the trees as she and Saul traveled toward Paradise. She was glad she'd brought along a sweater when she felt the cool breeze kick up. "Should be snowing soon, *jah?*" She shivered slightly.

"*Ach*, I'm sorry, Sarah. I should have considered you might get a chill. I should've hitched up the other buggy." His lips turned downward. "*Kumm*, scoot closer. I'll keep you warm, *schatzi.*"

Sarah sighed contentedly as Saul draped his arm around her and pulled her near, but guilt still nibbled at her. How was she going to make this work out?

"Who are you planning to meet today?"

"Truda. You don't know her."

"Is she from our district?"

"No."

"How long have you known her?"

"For a while. Since before we married." She hoped Saul wouldn't detect her vagueness.

"You'll have to introduce me to her."

"Uh, *jah.*" What would Saul say when he discovered she was an *Englischer?* They were allowed to converse with the *Englisch*, but close relationships were frowned upon. Fortunately, he hadn't asked any more questions. Perhaps he had something else on his mind at present.

"I will drop you off so you can meet your friend. When I am finished getting what I need at the hardware store, we can have dinner. How does that sound?"

Sarah nodded. "*Gut.*"

As soon as Saul dropped Sarah off at the restaurant they'd be dining in later, she spotted Truda. Her friend was already seated at one of the tables in the diner. She released a thankful sigh when her beloved drove out of sight. Their relationship had been coming along so well, she didn't want to mess it up. But perhaps some things were more important than smooth sailing. Maybe God had some storms, tempests even, planned for their future. Or maybe she was simply overreacting.

Sarah neared the table where her friend awaited her presence. They usually met at a small table in the corner for maximum privacy. As the bishop's daughter, Sarah couldn't afford to get caught so they always proceeded with caution.

"Was that your husband?" Truda's face brightened.

"Uh...*jah*."

Truda chuckled. "I know the feeling. You haven't said anything to him yet, have you?"

Sarah shook her head. "No. I'm frightened. I don't think he'll respond well. He is Amish through and through. I don't think he'd ever want to leave." Sarah bit her fingernail.

"And you?"

"I want the truth. I want to know that I have a purpose in living. That God has a plan for me. I want to know this God I've been reading about. He sounds so different than what I've always been taught."

"And so He is. Shall we begin our Bible study?" Truda reached her hand across the table and Sarah grasped it. They'd always began each Bible study with prayer.

When Sarah lifted her head, she felt a renewed sense of peace. She placed a hand over her abdomen when the babe inside suddenly moved.

"You are getting big. How much longer do you have?"

Sarah smiled. "Just a few more weeks. I can't wait to see what this little one looks like."

"I bet your husband is excited."

"*Jah*, he is. You should see him when the *boppli* moves. He will put his hand on my belly and talk to him. I think the *boppli* knows his *vadder* because he pushes on Saul's hand."

"He?"

"Or she. We don't know yet." She rubbed her abdomen.

Truda tapped her Bible, changing the subject. "Do you plan to tell your husband?"

"About our Bible studies?" She continued at Truda's nod. "I want to, but I...I just don't know. What do you think I should do?"

"What would God have you do? I think that's the more important question."

"Well, I'm supposed to submit to and reverence my husband. But I'm also supposed to follow *Der Herr*."

"That is true. What if Saul forbids you to read your Bible? What will you do?"

Sarah felt the perspiration begin to bead on her forehead. "I think it would be difficult for me to not read it. This is my spiritual food, *jah*? If I don't get it, I will starve to death. But if he forbids me, he would say that I am disobeying him by reading it."

"Sarah, sometimes disobedience is okay. You know that, don't you? God says we ought to obey Him rather than man. A husband is not God. So if a man tells you to do something contrary to the Word of God, what must you do?"

"I must obey God."

"Some have paid dearly for their obedience to God. Our Anabaptist ancestors were proof of that. They stood up for God's Word, but many of them lost their lives for it. Are you prepared to risk everything for Him?"

Sarah covered her face with her hands. This was all so much to think about. What would it mean for her and Saul's relationship? For their *boppli*? "I need to pray, I think."

"That is a good idea. It looks like we won't have time to study today. Your husband will be back soon, correct?"

Sarah nodded.

"Would you like me to pray with you before I go?" Truda took a sheet of paper from her Bible and handed it to Sarah. "Before I forget, here are the chapters I'd like you to study this week. We can discuss them later when you are alone, *jah*? I should go soon."

Sarah nodded in appreciation and they both bowed their heads to wrap up their session. Truda would need to leave before Saul returned. Although they didn't have time to study the Scriptures she'd read, Sarah valued every moment she was al-

lowed to spend with a fellow believer, someone she could talk
to about anything, and not have to worry about being rejected.

Saul scanned the restaurant in search of Sarah. He was glad
she'd joined him today, but she didn't seem her usual self. She
seemed reticent, as though she were keeping something from
him. Or perhaps doing something she didn't want him to know
about? There weren't any definitive clues, just a gut feeling he'd
had. She was nearing the time the *boppli* would come, so he
couldn't imagine why she'd make a trip into town alone. Unless
she was hiding something.

Fortunately, everything he needed at the hardware store had
been in stock and he'd found it quickly. He wanted to meet this
person Sarah spoke of. Why had she never mentioned her before? Saul found that strange. This whole situation seemed a
little odd, in fact.

Saul spotted Sarah and an *Englischer* at a table in the corner. Why hadn't she said her friend was *Englisch*? Upon further
observation, Saul noted their posture. Sarah and the *Englisch*
woman were...*praying*? He took his time, so as to not interrupt.
And to spy, he admitted to himself. There was nothing wrong
with him knowing his wife's activities, was there? Sarah's
friend discreetly slid a black book from the table and placed it
into the purse beside her. That's when Saul's jaw dropped.

No.

"Sarah?" Her name was all he could manage.

Sarah's surprised countenance became guilt-ridden. "*Ach,* Saul. I...I didn't realize you'd be back so soon." She fumbled over her words. "This is my friend Truda that I was telling you about."

"It is nice to meet you, Saul. I've heard so much about you," the Englischer said.

Saul's eyes met the woman's and he noticed her distinct Amish accent when she greeted him. *This woman is ex-Amish.* He'd heard numerous stories about people who had left the faith. None of them were good. They'd either gotten caught up in a terrible sin or they became proud, claiming to be saved. Either way, they'd become worldly like this *Englisch* woman with her head uncovered and hair down. Sarah did not need friends like this. She would attempt to persuade her away from their People – that is, if she hadn't already.

Saul hadn't said anything to the woman, but simply nodded. He was certain he conveyed his warning through his eyes. This woman had no business speaking with his *fraa* without his consent.

Sarah spoke up awkwardly. "Goodbye, Truda."

The woman smiled tenderly at Sarah and briefly glanced at Saul before exiting the restaurant. When she'd gone, Saul sat across the table from Sarah. His *fraa* was quiet. Much too quiet. Was she waiting for him to say something? This was not the place to begin a conversation of the sort they were sure to have. It would have to wait.

"Did you find everything you needed at Beiler's?" Sarah asked, attempting to sound casual.

He reached over and loosely grasped her hand. "*Jah.*" He was too addled to speak much. The truth was, he was worried. Who knows what kind of lies that *Englisch* woman told sweet Sarah. Women were known to be easily deceived, just like Eve in the Garden of Eden. But Adam hadn't protected his *fraa*, and Saul realized he hadn't protected Sarah either. Not only was he concerned, he was frustrated with himself. Why hadn't he seen this until now?

Other than the meals they'd shared when they first married, Saul determined this was one of the quietest they'd ever had. Normally, they spoke to each other about anything and everything during meal time. But not today. With each minute that ticked by, Saul grew more anxious.

NINE

*A*s soon as she exited the buggy, Sarah headed to the *dawdi haus.* This was not good. Saul had spoken a total of five words to her since Truda had left the restaurant. *He knows.* What other explanation could there be? What would she say to him?

For I am not ashamed of the gospel of Christ: for it is the power of God unto salvation to everyone that believeth...Lord, help Saul believe.

Her heartbeat quickened as she heard Saul's boots scuff across the back steps. The door slowly creaked open, as though emphasizing the present foreboding tone. Saul's heavy presence was overwhelming, especially since his breath lay hot on her neck. Sarah turned around to give him what he wanted.

Just one kiss. One slow, sweet, frustratingly wonderful kiss. Ever since Saul had informed her that they would wait to share the intimacies of the marriage bed until after the *boppli* was born, kissing seemed more like torture. But now, what would happen? Would they ever have a normal husband-wife relationship?

Sarah took a deep breath. Sooner or later they would have to discuss what had happened today. She hesitantly forged ahead. "What did you think of Truda?"

"I think you already know." Saul frowned and stepped away.

Sarah needed to get off her feet, so she beckoned him into the living room. As soon as she sat down on the couch to relax, the *boppli* moved inside her womb. Could the little one feel the tension too?

"We need to talk." She sighed.

Saul nodded in silent agreement.

Sarah wished he'd say something. She didn't want to confess everything she'd ever done wrong according to the *Ordnung*. She closed her eyes and offered a brief prayer for guidance.

"Have you been reading an *Englisch* Bible?" Saul's intense blue eyes met hers.

"*Jah.*"

"I knew it. You know that is against the *Ordnung*. Next you're going to tell me you got saved, right?" He huffed.

"Saul, please don't be upset." She lightly caressed his forearm.

He moved her hand away. "Don't be upset?" His voice raised an octave. "You've been sneaking out to meet some *Englischer* behind my back and you don't want me to be upset!"

"I knew her before we married. We've been friends for a while." Sarah thought of Truda. She had met her at a desperate time in her life. She'd just discovered she was in the family way with Saul's *boppli*. And she'd heard Saul had an *aldi* in a different district. Her parents didn't know and she was deathly afraid to tell them. She'd sat there in the diner alone, unable to stop the incessant flow of tears. That's when Truda approached her and spoke to her in Pennsylvania German, their native tongue. She hadn't expected the *Englisch*-dressed woman to speak her language, and she'd never met any former Amish.

Truda shared God's love with her and promised that she wouldn't have to do it alone. Even if her folks rejected her, even if Saul rejected her, God never would. And Truda offered to take her in if things didn't work out at home. Her words had given Sarah hope and courage to share her news with Saul and her folks.

Not only had her folks accepted her pregnancy, but Saul had agreed, although reluctantly, to marry her. God had been so good. Surely he would help them get through their present dilemma.

"Saul, if you'd just listen to what I have to say. We don't have to be Amish to go to Heaven–"

"Now you don't want to be Amish? Well, this is just wonderful," he said sarcastically. "I take a *fraa* and then she's shunned for the rest of our married lives. Have you thought this through, Sarah? Do you realize what you are doing? You must stop this talking now. I will not allow this speech in our home."

"You…you won't allow me to talk about *Der Herr*?" Sarah's mouth hung open.

Saul took her hands in his, his eyes beseeching. "Please, Sarah. For us. I beg you not to do this. You don't realize what this will mean for our family."

Oh, Saul looked so forlorn. Sarah pondered for a moment... Would she really be able to go through life as a silent believer? Could she just keep her mouth closed and watch those around her die in their sins, thinking their good works were earning them salvation, and allow them to slip into an eternity of Hell? Her husband, her children, her folks? *Jah*, they might despise her now, but what if they listened? What if they believed the Gospel of Christ and became saved? Didn't she have to at least try? How could she stand before God someday not having done her utmost to pull others from the fire? No, she couldn't do that. Ever.

"Saul, I need to talk to you about this. Please, I need you to listen to me."

"You want me to eat the forbidden fruit too, ain't so? No, I can't. I won't." He shook his head defiantly.

"These rules we follow are man-made. We don't need them to–"

"Enough! I won't hear any more."

Tears pricked Sarah's eyes. What could she do now?

"I will not tell your *vadder* about this. As long as you keep this to yourself, he will not know." Saul abruptly rose from the hickory rocker.

A moment later Sarah heard the back door slam. She buried her face in her hands and didn't attempt to stop the rush of tears that fell freely down her cheeks. It was the worst thing that could ever happen.

Saul had rejected the Truth.

TEN

It was getting close. Sarah felt her abdomen contract for the fifth time in the last half hour. Saul had left for work just a little over an hour ago. She'd awakened this morning feeling ill, but didn't want Saul to worry so she'd said nothing. Of course, she hadn't realized that the *boppli* might be coming. It was still a couple of weeks yet until her due date and the midwife had said most first *bopplin* arrive late. Another pain rippled across her midsection.

She really should go next door and inform *Mamm* so she could call the midwife. But she felt weak. *So weak.* Is this how she was supposed to feel when about to have a baby? Was this normal? She didn't know. Sarah tried to recall what she'd read from the book the midwife had loaned her. She couldn't remember anything about feeling sick or weak. *Something has to be wrong.*

Sarah forced herself from the couch, but as soon as she did, a dizziness swept over her. This was not good. Her breath came in short gasps and she immediately fell back onto the couch. There was no way she could make it over to *Mamm's*.

Please help me, Lord. I can't do this alone.

A knock on the back door startled Sarah.

"*Kumm!*" she called with all the strength she could muster in her feeble voice. She wished it were Saul, but she knew it wasn't. He would have just walked in without bothering to knock.

She heard the door hesitantly creak open. A female voice called out, "Sarah?"

Truda is here? "*Jah*, I'm in here!" Sarah felt like crying tears of joy.

Truda appeared in her living room and raced to the couch in short order. "I was in the neighborhood and–" she stopped midsentence when she saw Sarah's countenance. "Sarah, what's wrong? You look ill." Truda's worried expression mirrored her own.

"The *boppli*." Sarah panted.

"Do you need me to call someone? I could call 911."

"*Nee*. Saul. Please just call Saul." Sarah pointed to a small desk up against the wall. "His number is there, on a business card."

Truda removed her phone from her purse and quickly placed the call. Sarah could only imagine what Saul was thinking as he spoke to Truda. No matter. She had been an answer to her prayer.

"Okay. He's on his way. Is there anyone else you'd like me to call?"

"The midwife. Look for a paper with a number for Fannie."

"Got it. Do you want to talk to her?" Truda held her phone out.

Sarah nodded, taking the phone from Truda once she'd dialed the number. "Fannie, the *boppli's* coming!"

It seemed as though a million thoughts fought for a place in Saul's mind as he urged his horse toward home. *What was Sarah's friend doing in our home? I told Sarah not to have any more contact with her.* It grieved his heart to think his wife was stepping out from under his authority – it was like giving the devil permission to bring evil upon them.

After he'd gotten over the initial shock, he thought about their little one on its way. His heart leaped with joy at the thought of seeing their *boppli* for the first time. Would it be a boy or a girl? He admitted that when he first learned of Sarah's predicament, he wanted nothing to do with a baby. But as he and Sarah eventually learned to love each other, he found that his love for their *boppli* grew as well. Now, instead of a curse, he considered this baby a blessing.

As Saul attempted to hurry the horse on, he determined this had to be the longest thirty minute drive he'd ever taken.

Saul's heart stopped. The last thing he expected to hear when he stepped through the door was the cry of a newborn *boppli*. The baby was here! Unable to contain himself, he burst through the kitchen and past the living room. Once he reached the bedroom door, he'd slowed his pace and took a deep breath to calm his racing heart.

He stepped into the bedroom. Truda, Fannie, and Sarah's mamm all turned at his presence and smiled. The women must've sensed their need for solitude because they all abruptly exited the room and closed the door behind them.

Saul and Sarah locked eyes. Never had he thought he'd be able to love any woman as much as he'd loved Chloe Esh, but he was wrong. His heart yearned for Sarah. Even more so when he noticed the tiny miracle – their *boppli* – suckling at her breast. He examined the small bundle in awestruck wonder and softly placed a kiss on Sarah's lips. *"Ich liebe dich."*

Sarah's smile broadened. "We have a *maedel*."

His eyes widened. "We do?" He glanced at the baby, then back to his *fraa*. "I'm sure she's *schee* like her *mamm*."

Sarah blushed momentarily, then carefully removed the infant from her breast. She gently held the *boppli* out to its *vadder*. Saul hesitantly reached for his daughter, uncertain whether he was up for the delicate task.

"I hope you don't mind. I already named her. We can still change it if you'd like."

Saul intently studied the newborn in his arms with fascination. Did the two of them really make this precious little person? He smiled when the baby's tiny hand grasped his finger. He could hardly peel his eyes away from the beautiful *boppli*.

Saul briefly raised a brow to Sarah. "What is her name?" His captivated gaze lowered once again to the baby he held.

"Amanda Chloe Brenneman."

Saul's jaw went slack. "You...you want to name her after Chloe?"

Tears pricked Sarah's eyes. She nodded unequivocally.

Saul stared at his *fraa* in pure astonishment. "You really are an amazing woman, Sarah Mast Brenneman."

ELEVEN

*L*ittle Amanda Chloe was perfect in every way, Saul decided. She had been a *wunderbaar gut boppli* these first few weeks. She cried very little – only when she was hungry, tired, or needed to be changed. It seemed she slept most of the time, which was good for Sarah.

He'd noticed Sarah had been more tired than usual, but his *vadder* had told him it was normal. Not only was she recovering from giving birth, but she was constantly providing nourishment for their little one. Oftentimes she would wake in the middle of the night to feed and change the *boppli*.

While Saul appreciated all these things, he had to admit he was feeling a little neglected. Sarah used to spend her free time with him, but now the baby continually required her attention. He knew it seemed selfish, but in truth, he missed his *fraa*. And their dates.

They had visited many of the covered bridges in Lancaster County and kissed under each one. Every outing they'd gone on, they'd learned more about each other. Saul had come up with a fun way for them to get to know each other. On each date, they would share three things about themselves that were unknown by the other spouse.

He now knew Sarah's favorite color was orange because it reminded her of the morning sun peaking over the eastern horizon – a new day filled with promise. He found out that she was afraid of clowns because she'd had a bad experience as a small girl. She secretly liked to listen to country music, as did he. One time they'd even turned the radio on and danced to a love song. Of course, they'd both felt guilty afterward. Saul still had his radio from *rumspringa*. Radios were allowed, as long as they were powered by batteries and as long as they used them to listen to proper things like the weather forecast. Listening to music was frowned upon. And dancing was definitely *verboten*.

Saul eyed Sarah as she emerged from the bedroom. "Is the *boppli* sleeping?"

"*Jah*, now that she has a full tummy." Sarah smiled.

Saul pulled her down next to him on the couch. "I miss you." He slipped his arm around her and pulled her close.

"You miss me?" Sarah giggled.

"Well, *jah*, I don't get much time with you anymore." He stuck out a pouty lip.

Sarah leaned over and kissed his cheek. "Saul Brenneman, are you jealous of your *dochder*?"

He grinned sheepishly. "Just envious. I wouldn't mind being in your arms for hours every day."

She playfully slapped his arm. "You'd go crazy staying home that much. You'd get bored after a half hour and go out to work."

He moved a stray hair away from her face. "You're probably right. But I really do miss you."

"Well, I'm here now...and so are you."

"Right." He smiled and leaned over, pressing his lips to hers.

"Sarah?" A quiet voice called from the kitchen a few moments later.

Saul and Sarah immediately broke apart and Sarah hastened to re-pin her *kapp* in place.

Sarah's younger sister's face turned three shades of crimson when she entered the room. "Oh, I'm sorry! I should have knocked."

Sarah shot up from the sofa. "No, we were just..." She turned to Saul, then back to her sister. "Uh, did you need something, Judy?"

"I didn't want to wake the *boppli*," her sister explained. "That's why I came in quietly... It's *Dat*, Sarah. He doesn't look *gut*. *Mamm* thinks somethin's wrong with him."

Saul cleared his throat and stood up as well. "Does he need a driver to take him to the hospital?"

"*Nee*, Simon called already," Judy said. "*Mamm* asked if you could come tend to the *kinner* while she goes to the hospital with *Dat*."

"*Jah*, but the *boppli* just went to sleep." Sarah glanced at Saul.

"I can stay here with Amanda Chloe. I'll bring her over when she wakes up," Saul reassured.

Sarah nodded appreciatively, then motioned to her sister. "Let's go."

Sarah paced the kitchen floor of her folks' home, her conscience plaguing her with regret. What if her father died? She hadn't been a good witness for her Saviour at all. What if she never had another chance to share God's wonderful love with him? Even if he wouldn't listen, she'd have at least done her best. The results were up to *Der Herr*.

Dear God, please don't let Dat *die. Please give me another chance to share Your love with him.*

Before her *mamm* had left with her *vadder*, her mother had said she thought her father had a stroke. Sarah didn't know much about strokes, but she knew they were not good and that people sometimes died from them. When she'd seen her *vadder* sitting in the car before they drove away, she noticed he looked quite pale and seemed unusually quiet.

Sarah thought of her father and the influence he'd had over her life. He'd always been a *gut* father, she'd thought. Although he was strict, he had always treated his family and community with kindness and only dealt out punishment when warranted. But simply being a kind person did not win favor with God. Being a bishop wouldn't put him in God's good graces, either.

How would she be able to share that fact with her father? How could she make him see that the Amish religion was not the path to Heaven? There was only one path – only one way – and that was through Jesus. But if her own husband would not hear her, there was a good chance her bishop father wouldn't listen, either. Nevertheless, her conscience continued to implore her to share the Truth with him. She had to. She didn't know how or where she'd be able to share it, but she must.

As Sarah walked the corridor to her father's hospital room, she silently prayed for wisdom. Other than sharing the news of her pregnancy with Saul and her *daed*, this was one of the most nerve-wracking moments of her life. If her father rejected the Truth, the consequences could be devastating – not only for her father on judgment day, but also for her present life with Saul and Amanda Chloe.

Trust in the Lord with all thine heart, and lean not unto thine own understanding. In all thy ways acknowledge him and he shall direct thy paths. Sarah sucked in a deep breath. *Okay, Lord, I'll trust You. But I'm really scared right now.*

She stood in the hallway and glanced down at the small paper in her hand to be sure she'd found the correct room number, then reluctantly pushed through the door. Sarah's heart somersaulted when her eyes beheld her father's weakened condition. He appeared so frail and fragile, hardly like the strict leader of a large district. Perhaps his heart would be open now. Was that the reason for the whole episode? Was God paving the way for her father to hear the Gospel and accept Christ? A burst of fresh courage compelled her onward.

Sarah's mother turned when she neared her father's bed. "They just gave him some medication, so he'll probably be getting drowsy soon," she informed her.

Sarah nodded. "Did they say what's wrong with him?"

"*Jah.* It was a stroke. He's lost use of his left arm and some of his facial muscles are paralyzed as well. They said there's a good chance that he will regain use of his left side, but it will take time."

Tears pricked Sarah's eyes. It was difficult seeing her father, the man that had always been the tower of strength for her family and their People, in such a helpless state. Would one of the ministers step in and fulfil his duties while he was ill?

Her mother lightly touched her arm. "I'm going downstairs to call your brother. Is Saul here with you?"

"*Nee*, I came alone. Saul's with the *boppli.*"

Sarah's glance returned to her father when her mother exited the room. She took a seat in the chair next to his hospital bed and prayed silently.

"How's that *boppli* doing?" Her father's slurred speech startled her.

A smile formed across her lips. "*Dat.* I thought you were sleeping." She lightly grasped his hand. "Amanda Chloe is *gut.* How are you feeling?"

"Tired." His fatigued eyes evidenced the truth of his words.

Sarah realized she'd better say her piece before her father drifted off to sleep and she lost her chance. And her nerve. "*Dat*, I'm really concerned about you. I'm so glad *Der Herr* spared you. But what if you had died? Aren't you afraid that you might not go to Heaven?"

Bishop Mast patted his daughter's hand in reassurance. "Let's not worry about something that didn't happen. *Der Herr* is the only one who knows where I'll end up. I've done my best to serve Him. Hopefully, that will be enough when my time on this earth is over."

"But *Dat*, Jesus shed His blood to take your sins away. He is the only one that can save you. Following God's commandments and the *Ordnung* are good, but only Jesus can save us from Hell." She locked eyes with her father. "You *can* be saved and know it, *Dat*. Just ask Jesus to–"

"Sarah! Where did you hear these things? Someone has been filling your head with lies."

Sarah thought she'd heard him trying to cluck his tongue. "*Nee, Dat*. They're not lies. *Der Herr* says in His Word–"

"*You* have been studying the Scriptures? Sarah, you know that is *verboten*. Why have you done this?"

"*Dat*, please just hear me out. This is important. What if you don't get another chance?"

"Sarah, you must stop your babbling at once! Your worldly ways have affected you in more ways than I thought. First, you were in the family way out of wedlock, and now you're turning against the *Ordnung* and your family? And now you think you know more than the leaders *Der Herr* put over you?"

"*Nee, Dat.* That is not how it is."

"You must repent of these things." When Sarah shook her head in defiance, her father pointed to the door. "Leave now."

"But, *Vadder...*" Sarah realized it would be pointless to argue. He wasn't going to listen to her, she'd messed up too many times for her father to look beyond her mistakes. She meekly nodded, stood up from the chair, and quickly exited the room before her tears fell full-force.

TWELVE

*S*aul glanced at Sarah as she held the *boppli* in her arms. She had been a great *mamm* to little Amanda Chloe. He realized he couldn't have found a better woman to marry. He thanked *Der Herr* that he and Sarah now got along wonderfully. No longer did he regret marrying her or their having a child together. They'd both grown by leaps and bounds since their courting days. The not-so-distant past seemed like years gone by, yet it had only been months.

But something wasn't right with his *fraa*. Sarah did not look her usual self tonight. She seemed different. Sad. Perhaps she was upset about her *vadder's* condition. Was she worried about losing him?

He'd probed her with questions after she returned from the hospital, but she was too upset to speak about it. She said he wouldn't understand. How *could* he understand or even attempt to help comfort her if he had no idea what she was feeling? Sometimes women just frustrated him.

Saul sighed when he heard someone at the door. Again. It seemed they couldn't get two moments of solitude lately. He felt like putting a 'Do Not Disturb' sign on their door like they had when they'd spent a night at a motel on one of their dates. The home he and his father were building for their little family – which would hopefully be growing even more by next year, couldn't come soon enough.

"I'll get it." He hopped up from the hickory rocker and plodded to the back entrance.

Saul frowned when he noticed Deacon Hershberger on their doorstep. Why was he here?

"Good evening, Deacon," Saul greeted.

The deacon nodded in silence. He peered over Saul's shoulder. "Is your *fraa* here?"

Saul blinked. "My *fraa*?"

"There are some matters that need to be discussed." The deacon frowned.

Oh no. There was only one reason Saul could think of why the deacon would like to talk to Sarah. But nobody knew about that. Or did they?

Saul gulped then nodded. He led the way to their small living room.

The moment his eyes met Sarah's, he knew. She had told someone. "Sarah…" his forlorn voice trailed off.

Sarah nodded in understanding. "Hello, Deacon Hershberger. Would you like a glass of tea?" she offered.

"*Nee.* I will say my piece, then I'll be on my way."

Saul offered the man a seat, but the deacon chose to remain standing.

"Sister Sarah, it has come to my attention that you are attempting to lead the flock astray. Is it true that you are reading an *Englisch* Bible and claim to be saved?" The deacon's lips pursed together.

"I have accepted Jesus as my Saviour, *jah*." She didn't flinch.

Saul was taken aback by Sarah's boldness and confidence. However, he wished she would have denied it.

"You must stop speaking to others about this," the deacon continued.

"I cannot and will not stop speaking when God tells me to," Sarah declared.

"So now you are claiming that *Der Herr* speaks to you," the deacon said wryly. "Are you refusing to obey my orders and the *Ordnung* of our church?"

Sarah glanced at Saul again. "Only when it goes against what God says in His Word."

"Very well. I'm certain you realize what this means, being the bishop's *dochder*. Sarah Brenneman, you are now under the *Bann*. If you choose to repent of your insubordination, you will be received back into the flock. You have six weeks to think long and hard about the consequences of your choice. If you refuse to repent after that, you will be permanently excommunicated." He then turned to Saul. "Do you share her beliefs?"

Saul shook his head. "*Nee.*"

"This will be difficult for you as well, I'm afraid. You must shun your *fraa*. She is not to eat with you. She is not to sleep in the same bedroom as you. You may not receive anything from her hand. Communication must be minimal." The deacon looked sternly at Saul. "Do you understand?"

Saul nodded soberly.

"If these orders are not followed, you will be put in the *Bann* as well." The deacon nodded curtly, then showed himself to the door.

Saul stood speechless.

Sarah placed Amanda Chloe in her cradle beside the bed. The *boppli* slept peacefully, oblivious to turmoil going on around her. Innocence was a blessing.

She swiped at the tears that trailed her cheeks. Never had she imagined standing for Christ could be so difficult. She wasn't prepared for the betrayed look in Saul's eyes. She needed to talk to him. She needed him to realize that she wasn't abandoning him – not by choice. She still loved him.

When she stepped back into the living room, Saul frowned.

"Why, Sarah? Why did you have to go and tell people? Why didn't you keep this to yourself?"

"I had to tell my father. I didn't want him to–"

Saul's eyes bulged. "You told your father? Sarah, your father is the bishop. What did you think he would say? Did you expect him to approve of something he's been teaching *against* his whole life?"

Sarah exhaled. "I hoped he would listen and change his mind."

"Sarah, you can't reject our Amish ways and expect him – or me – to approve of it. You are on the path of destruction. You must turn from your rebellious ways. You must deny it."

She detected the frustration in his voice. "I can't deny the God who saved me, Saul. Don't you see that?"

"So where does that leave us? We live in the same house but act as though we're strangers?" Saul grasped a clump of his hair. "You said you didn't want me until you could have all of me. Well, all of me is here. I've waited like I said I would. I can wait another six weeks. But I refuse to wait my whole life. Sarah, I want us to be together. I want to share my love – all my love – with you."

"We still can."

"No, we can't! Didn't you hear the deacon? I will be shunned too." Saul released a breath. "Think about this, Sarah. Think about what you are doing to our family. Do you want Amanda Chloe to be an only child? Do you want the other children to treat her differently because her *mamm* is in the *Bann*? Do you want your husband longing for other women because he can't have you?"

"*I'm* not denying you. I'm not shunning you. You are shunning me. Don't make me out to be the bad person here. I'm doing the right thing." Sarah attempted to reassure herself that she was doing the right thing. It would be so much simpler if she just did as the leaders required. But she couldn't.

PART TWO

Hannah's Vocabulary

Afore – before

Aks – ask

Aw – all

Awfuw – awful

Awfuwy – awfully

Awm – arm

Awready – already

Betto – better

Da – to

Dat – that

Eben – even

'er – her

Fink – think

Fiwst – first

Fought – thought

Gots – have

Hab – have

Hafta – have to

Hewp – help

Howd – hold

'im – him

'imsewf – himself

Knowed – knew

Lib – live

Mawied – married

'member – remember

Neber – never

'nother – another

Onwy – only

'posed – supposed

Pway – pray

Pwayed – prayed

Pwayin' – playing

Pwibate – private

Thewe – there

Tickoes – tickles

Watched – washed

Webi – Levi

Weft – left

Wies – lies

Wif – with

Wight – right

Wike – like

Wips – lips

Witto – little

Wong – long

Wook – look

Wowd – world

Wub – love

Wyddie – Lyddie

Wying – lying

Ya – you

THIRTEEN

*C*hloe Hostettler removed the last batch of cookies from the oven and placed them on the cooling rack. She dabbed her forehead with a handkerchief and stuffed it back into her apron pocket. After glancing at the clock on the wall, she decided there would be enough time to visit with her long-time friend, Danika Yoder. It was time she told somebody her news. She had been keeping her secret for weeks now and she was sure she would just burst at the seams if she didn't tell someone.

"Ruthie, do you mind watching the *kinner* while I pay a visit to Danika? I shouldn't be gone more than a couple of hours." Chloe was thankful that Ruthie often came over to help her out with the chores. Hannah and Lyddie absolutely loved their aunt, and they were thrilled every time she visited. She often asked Chloe's advice on matters of the heart and she was happy to provide it for her younger sister.

"*Nee*, I don't mind at all." Ruthie's sweet smile glistened off her freckled nose.

"Great! You are a *wunderbaar schweschder*." She quickly planted a kiss on her sister's cheek, then hugged each of the children and explained that she would be back soon. The girls squealed with delight when she informed them that Ruthie would be their temporary caretaker. "And if Levi comes in from the field, let him know that I'll be back in time for supper." Chloe buzzed out the door and set off on foot to visit Danika.

The weather was a bit warm for spring and Chloe thought the clouds hinted of rain, although Levi hadn't mentioned the prospect when he quoted the Farmer's Almanac earlier in the week. It seemed as though the emerging clouds brought with them a thick blanket of mist transforming the forest around her into a large sauna. As the tall pine trees swayed in the gentle breeze, she wondered if perhaps a thunderstorm would ensue. Chloe picked up the pace and hurried to meet her girlhood friend.

As Chloe ascended the steps of the Yoders' front porch, she was bombarded with memories of her childhood. She and her best friend Joanna Fisher, now Joanna Scott, often came to this very house to deliver honey for a widowed Mennonite woman named Naomi Fast. Joanna had become friends with the woman after Naomi rescued her from the throes of an abductor. Naomi then met the local herbalist, Philip King, who was an uncle to Danika. Naomi converted to New Order Amish and she and Philip married shortly thereafter. After Danika's parents had passed away, she came to live with Philip and Naomi and became their daughter by adoption. The King family now lived in a larger house across the road, next to the herb shop where Danika worked part-time.

"Chloe!" her friend greeted her with an embrace as she opened the door. "I didn't expect to see you today."

"*Ach*, I know. I have something to tell you." Chloe smiled as Danika's young son reached up for her to pick him up. Chloe held out her arms and the little guy leaped into them. "How are you doing today, Jake?" she asked him in Pennsylvania Dutch. The boy gabbed a string of words neither she nor his mother understood. They both shrugged their shoulders and laughed.

Danika's eyes widened. "Oh, I forgot to tell you. Joanna sent a letter the other day. She and Caleb will be on furlough sometime this fall or late summer and they're planning a trip out here. I'm so excited!"

"*Jah*, I got a letter too. We'll have to all get together for a meal while she's here. It'll be just like old times. Wouldn't it be something if they're here when Jonathan and Susanna's *boppli* comes?" Chloe was disappointed when her best friend had chosen to marry an *Englischer*, and not remain Amish. But she was glad that she had not yet joined the church, because if she had, she would have been shunned by their community. Although they weren't considered part of the Amish community, Joanna and Caleb came back to visit every now and then when they weren't on the mission field in Central America.

"That would be *wunderbaar*. Are you catching their baby this time?" Susie hadn't spoken to Danika concerning this pregnancy yet, but she figured Susanna would be requesting some herbs soon.

"*Gott* willing, *jah*."

"What were you going to tell me when you came in? Sorry, but I was so excited about Joanna coming that I had to tell you before it slipped my mind. I didn't mean to be rude."

"*Ach*, sometimes the things you say remind me of how *Englisch* you were when you first came to Paradise! No, you weren't rude. Sometimes I wonder how rude we must sound to *Englischers*." Chloe laughed.

"Well, yeah. We Amish may sound that way to one that doesn't understand our culture. Englischers seem to try to, as they would say, "sugarcoat" everything. The Amish, or perhaps German culture in general, tend to just speak their mind. They speak the truth as they see it," Danika offered.

"Perhaps we should attempt to be more tactful, at least around outsiders," Chloe said thoughtfully, then remembered her initial reason for the visit. "*Ach*, how easily we get sidetracked when we start jabbering. Since you are my best friend, I thought you might want to know that Levi and I are expecting another *boppli*." Chloe's smile lit up her whole face.

"Really? That's *wunderbaar*, Chloe! I guess I should tell you something too. Eli and I are in the family way again as well!"

Chloe eyed Danika's still-slim figure. "*Ach*, we must be due 'round the same time."

"I hope you'll still be my midwife," Danika said.

Chloe smiled and absently patted her flat belly. "Just as long as we don't go into labor at the same time, it should work out. Abigail Lapp has been assisting me lately and she's become pretty knowledgeable. Between the two of us, it shouldn't be a problem. Maybe I'll step up her training a notch or two. Ruthie's been a big help around the house, but I'm afraid that when her beau gets a notion to propose I may need to stay home more often."

"Do you really think she'll marry that *Englischer*?" Danika's eyes widened.

Chloe laughed, remembering that it wasn't so long ago that Danika was an *Englischer*. "Seems like it, *jah*. Ruthie says he's converting to the Amish way. His sister, Brooke, led him to Christ a year and a half ago so I think his only qualm will be giving up modern conveniences."

"What was that little laugh for?" Danika asked curiously.

Little Jake wriggled in Chloe's arms and she let him slide down to the linoleum floor. He scampered into the other room and found some wooden building blocks to occupy his time. "I was just recalling a certain *Englischer* and how she adjusted to Amish life. Do you ever miss the *Englisch* world, Dani?"

"I'd be lying if I said I didn't. Some things more than others, for sure. I'd have to say that I miss the trips to the ocean most, though." Danika closed her eyes. "Just remembering the serenity of sitting on the seashore and listening to the waves crash. There's nothing like it in the world." Picturing the scene she had just described, her face held pure delight. "And, of course, I miss surfing."

"Have you and Eli taken a trip to the East Coast? There are plenty of nice beaches just a couple of hours from here. It's not California, but I'm sure it's just as *schee*. Ocean City has a nice beach, but there are way too many people there, in my opinion," Chloe offered.

"Oh, have you and Levi visited there?" Danika raised her eyebrows.

"*Ach, nee.*" Chloe blushed.

"Yeah, that's right. Didn't that guy from the other district take you there? What was his name again, Saul?" Danika recalled.

"*Jah.*" Chloe shook her head as she was assaulted by the bittersweet memories.

"Oh, I'm sorry to bring him up. I know he really hurt you." Danika chided herself.

Chloe batted a hand in front of her face. "That was a long time ago. *Gott* has healed my wounds. He brought me Levi and I couldn't ask for a better husband. He is *gut* to me and I love him very much." Chloe smiled. "So, have you and Eli been to the ocean?"

"No, Eli's always so busy at the shop. I know he would take me if I asked to go. Seems like he'll do anything to make me happy. He's such a *gut* man." Danika smiled at her good fortune, and then added, "I don't need the ocean to be content, though. I feel like I already have more blessings than I deserve."

"*Jah*, me too. *Gott* is *gut*, ain't so?" Chloe agreed. She took another sip of the peppermint tea Danika had served earlier, then glanced up at the clock. "Goodness, it's later than I thought. I'd better be off now."

"*Denki* for coming to visit and sharing your news with me. I bet Levi is thrilled," Dani said, as she walked her friend to the door.

Chloe slipped her coat on. "*Jah*. I think he's secretly hoping for a boy this time." She smiled, picturing her husband as a young shy schoolboy. "*Jah*, another little Levi would be nice."

A deafening roar of thunder booming through the sky interrupted their farewell.

"It looks like you'd better take our horse, it may begin pouring any moment," Danika suggested.

"I think you're right." Chloe bit her bottom lip. "I don't think Levi will be happy about it, though."

"I'm sure he'll understand this time."

"*Jah*, okay." Chloe embraced Danika one more time, and then quickly set off toward home once again.

FOURTEEN

*A*s soon as Chloe closed the barn door, the windows of Heaven burst open with a drenching rain. Thankful now that Danika loaned her a horse, she dismounted the large animal and led it into a nearby empty stall. She poured some fresh water into a bucket and placed some alfalfa hay into the manger.

She sighed when she thought about what Levi's reaction might be. He'd never approved of her riding horseback, didn't think it was proper for a *maedel*. They had had many disagreements in the past regarding this issue. While she still enjoyed riding the beautiful creatures, she gave up one of her favorite pastimes to honor her husband's wishes. It had felt so invigorating riding Danika's horse through the light rain and she remembered, once again, how much she missed it. She'd set out on foot, but decided the horse would be the quickest way to get back since the rain started sprinkling down. She hoped Levi was indoors already so he wouldn't confront her about the issue.

A rustling noise alerted Chloe to one of the stalls. Levi looked up from behind a stall gate, beads of perspiration accumulating on his forehead. "Chloe, I hadn't realized you were still out," her husband said as he set the rake against the railing of one of the back stalls and moved toward her. He leaned down and placed a gentle kiss on her cheek. Levi warily eyed the extra horse then raised an eyebrow, "Riding bareback again? Chloe, I thought you knew how I felt about that. Especially now that you're in the family way," he said, disappointment clearly in his tone.

"*Ach*, Levi. It was raining and Danika offered to let me borrow it," she attempted to explain. "I'd hoped you wouldn't mind it this once."

"Perhaps next time you can borrow the buggy instead," Levi suggested. He swung his arm around her shoulder and smiled. "Let's go in now, *fraa*. We need to get you warmed up. And I don't know about you, but I'm starving."

Chloe grimaced internally. She'd been at Danika's much longer than she had expected, so supper hadn't been made yet. Levi was probably imagining a delicious supper and she hadn't prepared anything. Oh, how she hated to disappoint her husband. Again. He'd been working hard out in the fields all day, the least she could do is have a hot meal ready for him. She chided herself for being so thoughtless, vowing to not let it happen again.

When they stepped into the house, nearly soaked from the short trot from the barn, a delicious aroma permeated the air.

Vegetable barley soup! It would go perfect with the bread she'd baked this morning. How thankful she was that her sister Ruthie had the forethought to start the evening meal. She would be sure to give her sister a big hug later and send her home with her favorite dessert. Ruthie had always loved chocolate brownies.

"You're here!" Ruthie exclaimed as they walked through the mudroom door. "I figured the rain might've held you up, so I threw together some simple soup. The girls have already eaten and I gave them a bath." She handed little Lyddie to her mother. Hannah reached up to claim a warm hug from her *daed*.

"That's perfect, Ruthie. *Denki*. I hope you're planning to stay and eat with us," Chloe said, noticing the already-set table for two.

"*Nee*, not today. Ethan's supposed to show up in about thirty minutes, so I really need to go." Ruthie's eyes brightened at the mention of her sweetheart. "He's starting baptismal classes tonight."

Chloe and Levi knowingly smiled at each other, and then at glowing Ruthie. Her *Englisch* beau was joining their Amish church district this fall, to her delight. Ethan fully intended to marry Ruthie this year and was willing to give up all of the modern conveniences of the *Englisch* world to do just that. He'd said there was nothing he wouldn't do to have Ruthie as his wife, and thus far he'd proved himself. Ethan would make a fine husband for her sister and Chloe was happy that she had someone that cherished her.

After Ruthie slipped out the door with a promise to return soon to claim her brownies, Chloe and Levi ascended the stairs and tucked the girls safely into their beds. Hannah looked expectantly at her mother, "*Mamm*, ya fink we'll hab 'nother *maedel*, or a *bu* for *Dat*?" Levi and Chloe both chuckled.

Levi placed a loving hand on Hannah's golden locks. "We'll have whatever the *Gut* Lord gives us. And a boy wouldn't be *just* for me, he would be for all of us. I love you and your *schweschder* just as much as I'd love a *sohn*, so don't you worry none. *Guten nacht, liebschen.*" He gently kissed his daughter's forehead, peeked into the crib where Lyddie was already fast asleep, and then clasped Chloe's hand to lead her downstairs.

"Our *dochdern* are precious." Levi sighed contentedly. "*Der Herr* is *gut.*"

Chloe smiled and nodded in agreement.

A peal of thunder tore through the sky as they sat down to enjoy their late supper. "*Ach*, it sounds like a bad storm," Chloe said anxiously.

"Don't worry, *liewi*. I'll protect you." Levi leaned over the table and placed a reassuring hand on her shoulder. "I like storms. They give us a chance to cuddle more." He winked and kissed her cheek.

"*Jah*, that would be nice." Chloe smiled. *That's my Levi.* It was one of the things she enjoyed most about marriage – Levi's strong arms wrapped protectively around her. He'd been protective of her for as long as she could remember, even before they'd started their long courtship. So much so, that Chloe's first beau had gotten annoyed with him. But Chloe never did. If anything, it endeared Levi to her heart even more. There was no doubt in her mind that her husband loved, cared for, and even cherished her. She couldn't be happier.

Levi finished the last of his soup and bread. "I think I'll go have a shower now."

"All right. I'll just wash up these dishes right quick." Chloe picked up the empty bowls and spoons from the table and made quick work of the kitchen chores.

Just as she finished washing the last few dishes, Levi entered the kitchen smelling fresh and clean. Chloe dried her hands and fell contently into his outstretched arms. He bent down and brushed her lips with his, lingering for a few moments. "We'd better have our evening devotions first, *jah?*" Levi reluctantly pulled back and guided her into the living room. They sat side by side on the plush brown sofa and he opened the Bible to the book of Proverbs.

"Trust in the Lord with all thine heart; and lean not unto thine own understanding." As Levi read chapter three of Proverbs, this one verse in particular stuck out to Chloe. Was it because of the frightening storm raging outside? She wasn't sure.

An hour later, while Levi softly snored under their wedding quilt, the verse persisted in her mind. She couldn't shake it. A flash of lightning brightened the room, followed by a loud clap of thunder. She brought the quilt up closer to her chin for comfort but for some reason sleep eluded her. Restless, she rose from the bed and decided to check on the girls. She padded down the hallway and peeked into their room. Thankfully, they were still sleeping peacefully. A horse whinnied loudly, and then Levi appeared in the hallway.

"Chloe, the barn's on fire! Stay with the girls and make sure they stay inside. I need to let the animals out." Levi buttoned up his shirt, pulled his suspenders over his shoulders, and quickly headed downstairs.

Chloe heard the back door slam shut and she ran downstairs after him. *Dear Lord, please keep Levi safe*, she prayed silently. Chloe opened the back door and stepped out onto the porch. She fiercely pulled the chain on the bell that hung from the fascia, alerting their neighbors to their distress. The fire raged in the barn and Chloe called out to Levi.

No answer.

A moment later, Chloe saw the horses running into the pasture out behind the barn. But where was Levi? She called out again, but suspected he couldn't hear her over the pounding rain.

Nathan Hostettler, Levi's older brother, showed up on horseback. "*Dat's* bringing the wagon," he hollered to Chloe, heading in the direction of the barn.

"Levi's still in the barn! Please help him, Nathan." Chloe fearfully cried out to her brother-in-law as she watched a large billow of smoke and flames rise up high into the sky.

"*Ach*, he shouldn't be in there." Nathan held his handkerchief under the pouring rain and tied it over his mouth and nose. He ducked his head, and then entered the flaming barn. A moment later, engulfed in smoke, two figures emerged from the barn. Nathan pulled Levi out from the barn door, both of them coughing like crazy. Levi collapsed on the ground several feet away.

"Levi!" Chloe cried out in horror and ran to him. Levi had ceased coughing and lay motionless. "Levi?" Chloe placed a shaking hand over her husband's hair, ashes falling through her fingers. She took her apron and gently wiped his sooty face. She leaned over his head, shielding him from the rain.

Levi's eyes fluttered open and he coughed uncontrollably. His eyes met Chloe's briefly and he reached a hand up to touch her stricken face. "*Ich liebe dich*," he breathed out, dropped his hand, and then shut his eyes once more.

"Excuse me, Ma'am." She heard an unfamiliar voice behind her. Chloe looked up to see two men in black uniforms and felt them ushering her a few feet away. She watched in shock as two emergency workers placed a clear plastic device over Levi's face. After several minutes, one of the men looked up at Chloe with disappointment etched in his features then hung his head. "I'm sorry, Ma'am."

Sorry? What is he sorry for? Realization slowly dawned as she read the attendant's face.

Oblivious to the sirens and the commotion around her, Chloe ran to where Levi lay, crumbled to the ground, and sobbed. "*Nee! Nee!* It can't be. I need him." She frantically reached out and shook Levi's shoulder with no response. "Levi? Levi? No!

Please, God, don't take him! Please," she begged. "Levi, don't leave me. Don't leave me!"

She forlornly glanced up into the faces of her father-in-law and Nathan standing by, tears streaming down her face uncontrollably. They, too, looked on helplessly.

Bishop Hostettler placed a hand on Chloe's shoulder. "He's gone, *dochder*. My *sohn* is…gone." Judah's voice cracked as he said the words and moisture formed in the corners of his eyes. "*Der Herr* has taken him home."

Chloe leaned over Levi's lifeless body and lovingly caressed his face. She placed one last resigned kiss on his cheek, laid her head on his silent chest, and wept. She couldn't stop the tears. How would she live without Levi? How could she do this alone? She placed a hand over the place their unborn *boppli* resided and thought of their two young *dochdern*.

Trust in the Lord with all thine heart; and lean not unto thine own understanding. The words came rushing back to her mind. She knew then and there that God was bringing her comfort and that somehow she had to trust Him.

"I'll try, Lord," she whispered into the wind. "I'll try."

FIFTEEN

"Where's *Dat*?" Hannah's innocent eyes mirrored her question. Chloe sighed. Levi had passed months ago and still her young daughter didn't seem to understand. She couldn't grasp the concept that he was gone permanently.

"Remember, Hannah? I told you that *Dat* went to live with Jesus after the barn caught on fire." Chloe glanced out the window to the newly built barn. The community rallied together shortly after the inferno to build a new barn for her family. Every day, meals were brought by members of their church district with words of sympathy and encouragement. And while those things were appreciated, she'd much rather have Levi's arms wrapped around her at night, his kind smile in the morning.

"But I want 'im to lib wif us. When's he comin' back? He's been gone too wong alweady," Hannah whined.

"Oh, *liewi*." Tears filled Chloe's eyes and she quickly brushed them away so her daughter wouldn't see. "He's not coming back. But someday we'll get to go see him." Oh, those words were still so difficult to say! *He's not coming back...*

"Can we go see 'im soon, *Mamm*? I miss 'im awfuwy bad." She stuck out her bottom lip to demonstrate her displeasure.

Chloe drew Hannah into her arms and pulled her close to her chest. "I do, too. But we have to wait until God says it's time before we can see him again." Movement from inside Chloe's belly caused Hannah to giggle.

"*Vas dat* my baby *bruder*?" she asked, wide-eyed.

"*Jah*, it was the *boppli*. But we don't know if it's a brother or sister." Chloe reminded Hannah.

"Will *Dat* get to see 'im?"

"*Jah*, he'll see him from Heaven."

"How do ya know *Dat* is in Heaben and not the bad place?"

"That is a good question." Chloe thought on how to best use this opportunity to share the Gospel with her curious daughter. "Do you remember when *Dat* read the Bible one night and told us about how Jesus died on the cross?"

Hannah wrinkled her little nose and put a finger on her chin, pondering her mother's question. "Oh, *jah*, I 'member. 'Twas awfuw sad."

"*Jah*, it was. But Jesus had to die to take away our sins," she explained.

"We can't go da Heaben wif our sins, ain't so?" Hannah asked.

"That's right, Hannah. You're such a *schmeart maedel*," she lovingly patted her hand. "Heaven is perfect, so there can't be any sin there."

"Do I gots sin?" Hannah's eyes grew wide at the possibility.

"The Bible says that all have sinned."

"I don't wanna hab sin. I wanna go da Heaben wif *Dat*." At that realization, tears sprung up in Hannah's eyes.

"Then ya gotta ask Jesus to save you and take your sins away."

"Can I aks 'im now, Mamm?"

"*Jah*, Hannah. You can do it right now." She smiled.

Hannah put her two small hands together and bowed her head. She opened one eye and peeked up at her mother. "Is it aw wight if I pway da Jesus in pwibate?"

Chloe chuckled. "*Jah*, that would be just fine. I'll go downstairs and start on lunch."

"*Denki, Mamm*." Hannah called back as Chloe walked out her bedroom door.

As Chloe stepped over the threshold of the girls' bedroom and closed the door, she sent up a brief prayer of praise and thanksgiving. God's hand was surely in this. And Levi would be happy to know that his death was a stepping stone to his daughter's salvation.

Chloe was happy to have some time away by herself. When Ruthie offered to watch the girls for her, she jumped at the chance. She knew she was in desperate need of solitude. It seemed since Levi's death, everyone had been hovering around her and, although she was thankful for their concern, she felt like she was suffocating. The lengthy buggy ride to Walmart in the fresh air was just what she needed.

Levi. Oh, how she missed her precious, kindhearted husband! She knew that people would be encouraging her to marry again, especially since she would have a new little one to care for soon. How could she even consider marrying another man? Wouldn't she be betraying Levi somehow? No. She decided she would remain a widow and single mother. But she did realize that children needed both a mother and a father. Perhaps her brother Stephen could be a sort of foster father to her children. *But he already has six* kinner *of his own.*

She pulled into one of the parking stalls at Walmart and tethered Winner to a nearby tree. Two other Amish buggies were parked as well, both from neighboring church districts as identified by their distinct markings. Chloe didn't know too many people from the other districts, but had met a few ladies at barn raisings and such. She secretly hoped that she wouldn't know anyone shopping today.

As Chloe stared at the seemingly endless bottles of shampoo, she plucked one off the shelf in front of her. She flipped open the cap and breathed in a whiff of the sweet-smelling fragrance and then turned the bottle around to view the ingredients list. Her friend Danika had taught her to do this, informing her that most health care products contained dangerous toxins. After reading the first few items that she was unable to identify, she quickly returned the bottle to its place on the shelf. *I think I'll stick to my homemade shampoo, at least I know what's in it.*

Her thoughts were interrupted by a piercing scream. A child in the next lane over was obviously not happy. She heard a male voice quietly attempting to calm the child down. She was almost to the end of the aisle when a small boy clad in a straw hat and suspenders toddled around the corner.

Chloe smiled and greeted the small fellow. "Hello there." The boy's large blue eyes somehow seemed familiar although she knew she'd never seen the little guy before. Perhaps she knew his mother. The little one blabbered on in Pennsylvania Dutch baby talk and she caught a word here and there. "Where's your *mamm*?" she asked the little boy in his native tongue.

"Nehemiah! *Ach*, there you are," the frantic father called out as he knelt down in front of his small son. "Don't you walk off like that again."

He lifted his head and the man's piercing blue eyes met Chloe's from under his straw hat. She would know those eyes anywhere.

Saul Brenneman.

"Chloe?" Saul's eyes widened in astonishment. "Is it really you?"

"*Jah*, Saul. How are you?" Chloe smiled.

"*Gut, gut*. You look *gut*." He raised his eyebrows, noticing her protruding belly. "When is the *boppli* due?"

"Eight weeks," she replied with a smile, gently rubbing her mid-section.

"I bet Levi's excited."

"*Ach*, you haven't heard?" Her eyes misted.

"Heard what?" He tilted his head to one side and lowered his eyebrows.

"Levi..." She fought for a breath. "He passed away six months ago. There was a terrible storm and lightning struck our barn. The fire...Levi inhaled too much smoke into his lungs...he didn't make it." A lone tear rolled from her eyelash and slipped down her cheek. She choked back a sob.

"*Ach*, Chloe. I'm so sorry for your loss." He knew it was improper, especially here in the middle of the store, but he found himself drawing her into his arms. He held her tight as the tears fell from her eyes. *Poor thing. She's going through this pregnancy all alone. Does she have any other children? What about them? Would they be raised without a father?* Oh, how his heart ached for his former sweetheart. *She must have been devastated when she lost Levi.*

He knew the feeling well. When he had lost Sarah a couple of years ago, he felt like the pain would never end. He vividly recalled how difficult it had been on him and the children. Ev-

ery day he'd struggled with regrets, and some days even breath-
ing seemed painful. But now it seemed that with every day that
passed, the pain eased a little more. He determined he would
help Chloe through her time of mourning.

"*Dat?*" Ten-year-old Amanda Chloe rounded the corner
with a shopping cart with his other two children. Saul quickly
released Chloe from his embrace, receiving a bewildered look
from his daughter.

Saul cleared his throat. "Amanda Chloe, meet Chloe Esh. I
mean, Hostettler."

Chloe shot him a curious look. "Amanda *Chloe?*"

"*Jah*, Sarah insisted we name her after you." Saul smiled. "I
lost my *fraa* two years ago," he explained.

Chloe frowned. "I'm sorry to hear that, Saul. She must have
been a *gut* woman," she said sincerely.

"She was."

Chloe held out her hand to his daughter. "Amanda Chloe,
it's very *gut* to meet you." Chloe gave the girl a genuine smile
that reminded Saul of their courting days.

"The *kinner* and I are going to have some lunch after this.
We'd be happy to have you join us." He smiled in anticipation.
*Oh, how nice it would be to share a meal with female com-
pany again. Especially with this lovely woman in particular,* he
thought.

Chloe hesitated for a moment. Ruthie *did* say for her to take
her time and enjoy herself. It had been so long since she'd had
a nice meal out. She and Levi rarely spent money to eat out.

Chloe glanced down at her black cape dress and remembered that she was still in mourning. *Would having a meal with Saul be considered inappropriate? It isn't as if it's a date or anything,* she reasoned with herself, *all of his children will be present.* "*Jah,* Saul. I'll have lunch with you and the *kinner.*"

"*Wunderbaar!*" he exclaimed, not bothering to conceal his excitement. "Do you still have some shopping to do?"

"*Jah,* but I could return later. Probably would be better since I need to buy some refrigerated items." She glanced down at her empty shopping cart. "Unless you still have more shopping to do."

"*Nee,* we're done. Let's go, then." Saul smiled at Chloe and she agreed as she followed him to the cash register. After walking out the door with the children in tow, he strode over to his buggy, which he realized was parked right next to Chloe's. Chloe walked around to the side of her buggy and placed her hand on the side rail to hoist herself up. Saul quickly went to stand behind her and placed his hand over hers.

"Please, Chloe. Ride with me and the *kinner.* There's no sense in taking two buggies." Chloe looked up into his kind eyes and for some reason a shiver went through her body. She nodded in agreement and followed him to his buggy.

As Chloe slid into the red vinyl booth next to two of Saul's children, she thought of her own two daughters at home. She knew Ruthie would take good care of them in her absence. She was glad that God had chosen to bless her and Levi with three children. Unfortunately, Levi would never get to meet this precious little one that she was carrying inside her womb.

Saul spoke, drawing her out of her musings. "How many *kinner* do you have, Chloe?" He pulled out a menu.

"Three including this one." She smiled and rubbed her bulging abdomen.

"*Des gut*." Saul wondered for a second. "Where are the other two?"

"At home. Ruthie is watching them."

"Ruthie? You mean sweet little Ruthie, your sister?" he chuckled.

"*Jah*, but she's not so little anymore. She's almost seventeen now." Chloe smiled.

"Seventeen? Wow, that makes me feel like an old man." He rubbed his full brown beard.

Chloe laughed. "*Jah*, I know what you mean."

"I remember when I met your family for the first time. Ruthie thought I was Saul of Tarsus." Saul laughed out loud, his blue eyes sparkling. "And I think Stephen wanted to pound me."

"*Jah*, I think you're right. Stephen was certainly overprotective of me." She smiled at the recollection.

"How is Stephen, by the way?" Saul wondered aloud, remembering their last encounter in the woods. It hadn't gone so well. Hopefully Stephen didn't still harbor bitterness toward him.

"*Ach*, he's *gut*. He married Anna Beiler and they have six *kinner*." She smiled again, thinking of her brother. "He's a *gut daed*."

Chloe and Saul continued to converse as they ate their meals. The children piped up every now and then asking Chloe questions. They all laughed a lot and soon their time together came to an end. Neither Saul nor Chloe wanted to part ways when Saul dropped Chloe back off at her buggy.

"I'd like to see you again, Chloe." Saul finally got up the nerve to say. "Is that possible?"

Chloe nodded, and then made a suggestion. "You and the *kinner* are welcome to come over for a meal."

"We'd like that. How does next Saturday sound?" Saul asked.

"*Gut*." Chloe smiled, already putting together a menu in her head.

"I will look forward to it." He gazed into her beautiful green eyes a little longer than he should. Finally, he returned to his buggy with the children and started toward home. Saturday couldn't come soon enough! Saul smiled in wonderment. Who would have thought that he'd have another chance with Chloe? God was indeed good.

Chloe burst through the door with bags in hand, humming a song unfamiliar to Ruthie. Ruthie lifted her eyebrows and looked curiously at her older sister. She looked happier than she'd been in months. "It looks like someone had a good time," Ruthie commented.

"*Ach*, Ruthie. You'll never guess who I saw at Walmart!" Chloe couldn't hide her smile if she tried.

"Okay, then tell me," she said excitedly.

"Saul Brenneman," Chloe attempted to say in a voice as calm as possible.

Ruthie's eyes lit up like a Christmas tree. "Saul?! As in blind Saul? Your old beau?"

"*Jah*," Chloe said nodding her head, suddenly bashful.

"Well? What did he say?" Ruthie was dying to know.

"I had lunch with him." Chloe smiled.

"You went on a date with Saul Brenneman?!" Ruthie asked in disbelief.

"*Nee*. No! No. It wasn't a date," Chloe attempted to clarify. "He had his *kinner* with him. He has one girl and three boys."

"Still sounds like a date to me." Ruthie's knowing smile told her sister she wasn't as naïve as she'd assumed. Her face suddenly became blank. "Wait a minute, I thought he was married."

"His *fraa* passed away. We didn't really have much time to talk about it. Or maybe he didn't want to say too much in front of the *kinner*. I don't know."

"Hmm...sounds like an opportunity," Ruthie teased. "So when are you going to see him again?"

"*Ach*, he's...I mean *they* are coming over on Saturday for supper." She began chewing on her nails nervously.

"I knew it! *Ach*, Chloe. I'm so happy for you!" Ruthie beamed. "So, is he still as handsome as he used to be?"

"Ruthie!" Chloe protested.

"Well, is he?" She wasn't giving up easily.

"No. He's even more handsome." She smiled, staring down at her shoes.

"I can't wait to tell *Mamm* about this!" Ruthie joshed, gauging Chloe's response.

"*Ach*, Ruthie! Don't you dare tell anyone," Chloe warned.

"I was just teasing you. I know it's not my place to tell," Ruthie assured Chloe and she let out a sigh of relief.

SIXTEEN

*S*aul flicked the reins on his buggy urging his horse to trot faster. His palms began sweating again at the thought of being with Chloe. He couldn't remember her looking more beautiful. His heart raced in his chest as he recalled their conversation at Walmart. Chloe was no longer married and neither was he. Losing Sarah had been difficult and he still missed his *fraa*, but he couldn't help but think that maybe God was giving them a second chance. *Does Chloe feel the same way? Is she ready for another relationship?*

"Chloe seems nice, *Daed*." Amanda Chloe interrupted his thoughts.

"*Jah*, she is." *In every way*, he thought.

"How do you know her, *Daed*?" She looked up at her father inquisitively.

"She used to be my *aldi*," he said.

"*Ach*, for real? What happened? How come you didn't get married?" she asked curiously.

"I married your *mamm*," he said a little too sharply, he realized.

"I know, but–"

"That's all you need to know."

"Oh." Amanda Chloe figured that by the tone of her father's voice, it would be best not to ask any more questions. But still, she wondered why he answered her that way.

Saul changed the subject. "So, what do you think she'll make for supper?"

"I don't know, maybe meat loaf or roast. I hope it's good, though." She smiled.

"I'm sure it will be *appeditlich*," he assured his daughter, then blew out a sigh when he realized where they were. He looked down the lane and spotted a large white clapboard house with a spacious wrap-around porch. Although he'd never been here before, he knew that this was the house that Levi had built for him and Chloe to live in. The house, with the exception of the oversized porch, was very similar to most Amish dwellings in the district. White paint, green shutters, six-paned windows. He glanced around and noticed the large barn that he assumed must have been recently rebuilt by the community after the fire Chloe described. The one that claimed her husband's life. He shuddered at the terrible thought. *Poor Chloe.*

Saul pulled up to a hitching post near the barn and tethered Chestnut to it. He helped Amanda Chloe down, and assisted her with her younger brothers. His eyes shined when he saw Chloe descending the steps on the back porch.

"You may put him in the pasture if you'd like," Chloe offered, pointing to a large grassy fenced-in area nearby. "But hurry, though. Supper's about ready."

Saul nodded and unhitched his horse.

Chloe turned to his children. "I baked some cookies a little while ago. They're in a basket on the table. I'm sure your *daed* won't mind if you have just one before supper." The children looked to their father for approval and Saul nodded. He gave Chloe a thankful smile, and then closed the pasture gate, walking alongside her to the house.

Chloe led the way to the kitchen table where her daughters sat patiently, looking warily at their guests. "Hannah, Lyddie," Chloe made sure the girls were paying attention before she continued, "this is Saul, Amanda Chloe, Timothy, Joel, and Nehemiah." She pointed out each one, and then informed Saul's family, "Hannah just turned four years old and Lyddie is two."

Saul put out his large hand and extended it to the small girls with a smile. "Very nice to meet you, girls. My Joel and Nehemiah are the same ages as the two of you."

Hannah smiled and shook his hand. "I knows *Enguish*."

"English, Hannah. Not anguish," Chloe corrected.

Lyddie only offered a blank stare.

Chloe laughed. "I don't think she knows what to make of you just yet." She turned to her youngest daughter, speaking sweetly. "It's okay, Lyddie. I don't think Saul bites...anymore." She gave him a teasing smile and he laughed out loud, recognizing her inside joke.

"Now you're going to scare her," he warned with smiling eyes.

"Just give her time. She'll come around," she reassured him. Chloe turned to Saul's children that now sat at the table. They were presently devouring the remainder of their treats. "How are those cookies?"

"Hey, may *dat* have one too?" Saul asked, reaching for a cookie.

"I don't think so," Chloe teased, playfully slapping his hand. "*Dat* has to wait till after supper."

Saul feigned disappointment by crossing his arms and jutting out his bottom lip.

Little Hannah glanced from Chloe to Saul, eyes wide. "Are you my new *Dat*?"

Saul coughed, and then looked to Chloe.

Chloe's cheeks flamed. "Oh, no, *liewi*. Saul is Amanda Chloe and the boys' *vadder*," she clarified, looking at Saul apologetically. But somehow, Saul didn't seem to mind one bit. Chloe walked to the stove to retrieve supper.

Saul's eyes brightened as Chloe set the meal on the table. "Did you make—"

"Fettuccini Alfredo? *Jah*, just for you."

Saul couldn't wipe the smile off his face as he gazed at Chloe in wonderment. "You are every bit as amazing as I remember you."

Chloe's cheeks immediately pinkened again at his compliment. "You haven't tried it yet. You might just change your mind." She laughed.

"I wasn't talking about the food." He flashed his gorgeous smile, and then noticed the children watching their banter. Saul quickly cleared his voice and regained his composure.

"Would you like to say the blessing?" Chloe asked, after setting down a large bowl of salad and fresh bread.

"*Jah.*" He bowed his head and the rest of the table followed suit. Soon everyone's plate was filled with delicious Italian fare.

"*Sehr gut!*" Six-year-old Timothy exclaimed with a mouth full of pasta.

"My sentiments exactly." Saul reached over, gave Chloe's hand a quick squeeze, and winked. "I won't need to visit Bella Italiano anymore. I'll just come here from now on."

"Oh, you will, huh?" Chloe said as she thought of the quaint Italian restaurant Saul had taken her to when they were courting. "How often do you eat there?" she asked curiously.

"The last time I was there was...with you." Saul looked her in the eye and held her gaze. "I'd like to go back very soon though."

Chloe gulped. Was he asking to court her again? *But Levi...* She would talk to her father-in-law, Bishop Hostettler, for his sage advice.

"Do you think Ruthie would mind watching your *kinner* again this Monday? I'm sure my *mamm* will love to watch my

kinner. She jumps at every chance she gets." He smiled, anticipating her answer.

"I...I don't know, Saul. I'll need to speak with the bishop
first," she said reluctantly, glancing down at her black attire. "I
can talk to him on Sunday when he comes over for–" She was
interrupted with a knock on the back door. "Let me get that."

Chloe opened the door to find her father-in-law on the stoop.
"*Hullo*, Bishop. What brings you by this evening?" She nervously clasped her hands together as she led him inside. What
would her father-in-law think of her entertaining a male guest?

"I was just driving by and thought I would say hello to my
grossdochdern." He glanced at the table. "I saw the buggy outside. Do you have a caller?"

"*Jah.* A family from Bishop Mast's district," Chloe said
as she and Judah entered the dining area. "Judah, this is Saul
Brenneman and his *kinner.*" She registered the concern conveyed in the bishop's eyes.

Saul stood up from the table and offered the older man a
handshake. "*Hullo*, Bishop Hostettler." Judah seemed to take
Saul's hand uneasily and gave a curt nod. "Would you like to
join us? Chloe's food is excellent."

Chloe took a deep breath, wondering just *what* the bishop
was thinking. Would Judah detect too much familiarity between the two of them? After all, she had lost Levi only six
months ago. And Levi was his beloved son.

"*Nee, denki, sohn.* Just wanted to greet my *grossdochdern.*"
He moved over to Hannah and Lydia and gave each of them a

hug. The girls merrily returned their *grossdawdi's* embrace. He arose and motioned Chloe to the back door. Chloe glanced back at Saul with an uneasy expression before exiting.

Once on the porch, Judah turned to Chloe. "I am concerned for you, *dochder*."

"I had planned to speak with you on Sunday," Chloe said quietly.

"This Brenneman fellow. I've heard...*things* about him in the past. Some not so *gut*. I don't want to see you hurt." The bishop rubbed his full graying beard, contemplating his next words. "I know you're lonely and you miss our Levi, but rushing into something is not *gut*."

"Yes, Judah, I do miss Levi. Very much so. And until I ran into Saul the other day in town, I didn't think I'd ever be interested in another man again." She blew out a breath sending her *kapp* string flying. "Saul and I have known each other for a long time and we used to court. He is now widowed, same as me. I know about his past. We had plans to marry before he found out about Sarah's situation. I didn't understand God's wisdom back then, but it's clear to me now. If I'd married him before, I would have never had a chance with Levi. I'm grateful that He gave me Levi and our *kinner* to love." She finished with tears in her eyes, rubbing her abdomen. "But now...Levi is gone. And Saul is here."

Judah seemed misty eyed as well. "Very well, *dochder*. This young man may court you. But you must wait out the full year of mourning until you marry, as is our custom." He paused for a moment. "Bishop Mast's district does not believe the same as we do and that brings me great concern as well. You and Saul will need to work some things out first, *jah*?"

"*Jah*. I won't be unequally yoked," Chloe agreed.

"If you would like for me to speak with him on the matter, let me know. *Guten owed*, Chloe." The bishop tipped his hat and descended the back steps.

"*Denki*, Judah," Chloe called as he paced toward his buggy. She turned around and sent up a quick prayer of thanks before she opened the door to go inside.

Saul looked up from the table, assessing Chloe's demeanor. "I hope everything is all right."

"*Jah*, it is. I'm sorry I took so long. I spoke with him about you. He's not opposed to me having supper with you." She sat back down at the table.

A wide smile stretched across Saul's face. "That's *wunderbaar*, Chloe."

"Aw, *Dat*. You're goin' to a restaurant and you ain't takin' us," Timothy protested, his large blue eyes mirrored his father's.

"*Nee*. Not this time, *sohn*." Saul winked at Chloe. "Besides, wouldn't you rather go to your *grossmudder's*?"

"I reckon." He shrugged.

Chloe stood up and began clearing the dishes from the table; Saul stood up to help. "You don't have to do that, Saul."

"I insist," he said. "Do you have some toys the *kinner* can play with?"

"*Jah*, in the living room," she said.

He called back to the table, "Amanda Chloe, please take the *kinner* to the other room to play while I help Chloe with the dishes."

Chloe gave Saul a puzzling look. *Levi never helped me with dishes.* Not a complaint, simply an observation.

He set the rest of the dirty dishes in the sink and turned on the water to rinse off the contents. "What's wrong?" he asked when he noticed her perplexed countenance.

"I don't expect you to help with women's work," she said, still in disbelief.

Saul turned off the water, dried his hands on a towel, and glanced toward the living room. He turned to look her in the eye. "You forget I've been on my own for two years. Besides, did it ever occur to you that maybe I'd like to help? I want to be where you are, Chloe." Saul leaned forward and gently kissed her cheek. When he found no resistance, he lifted her chin and brushed her lips with his. "I've been dying to do that all week," he whispered, both oblivious to the soft footsteps that entered the kitchen.

"I knowed you was my new *dat*!" Hannah exclaimed and threw her arms around his leg.

Saul smiled at Chloe and shrugged his shoulders. He knelt down and rubbed Hannah's little back. "I'm not your *daed*, Hannah. Your–"

"But ya hafta be," Hannah objected. "*Mamm* onwy kisses *Dat* on the wips. Ain't so, *Mamm*?"

"*Ach*, Hannah. You're supposed to be playin' with the other *kinner*," Chloe chided, her face flushed. *I knew I shouldn't have let Saul kiss me. Now I've set a bad example for Hannah.* Chloe groaned inwardly. *Lord, once again, help me to flee temptation.* She never thought she'd have to pray that prayer again, but here she was.

"But I got firsty, *Mamm*." She looked up with her large hazel eyes.

"Well, then, we'd better get you a drink of water." Saul opened the cupboard above where he stood and was pleased to find a small cup. He quickly filled it halfway with water and knelt down. He handed the cup of water to Hannah, who promptly gulped it down.

"*Denki*," she said, leaning toward Saul. A small hand hid the word she whispered in his ear, "*Dat*." Hannah then turned on her heel and happily rejoined the other children, leaving a smile on Saul's handsome face.

"What did she say to you?" A slow smile formed on Chloe's lips.

"Can't tell ya. You wouldn't want me to betray the confidence of a four year old now, would you?" Saul said defiantly.

Chloe sighed and put her hands on her hips, feigning exasperation.

"Hey, you're cute when you're mad." Saul winked, and then took a step toward her. "No more *kinner*. Now, where were we before we were interrupted?"

Chloe smiled and took a step back. "We better get these dishes done. The *kinner* will want dessert soon."

Saul chuckled. "You're right about that. I guess the dishes won't do themselves. Wash and rinse, or dry and put away?"

"I'd better dry and put away. You don't know where anything goes."

In no time, the adults were finished with dishes and joined the children in the other room. Saul sat on the couch and Nehemiah quickly left his toy and toddled toward him, reaching up his arms. Chloe watched from the rocker where she sat as he lovingly took his son into his arms and placed a kiss on the top of his head. The little one wiggled down, rejoined the other children, and found the small horse he'd been previously playing with.

As they sat observing the children, Chloe pondered when the best time would be to bring up the district differences. She vaguely remembered when the Hostettler district split and the Mast district began. At that time, there were few members in the Mast district, but other families had moved to the area and joined – Saul's family being one of them. The Yoders left as well, but soon rejoined the Hostettler district, paving the way for Eli and Danika to marry. She hoped the issue wouldn't be a source of contention between her and Saul.

"You appear to be in deep thought." She startled when Saul distracted her from her musings.

"*Ach, jah.* There's something I'd like to speak with you about later. Not tonight, though," she said.

"We'll have plenty of time to talk on our date Monday evening." He smiled and she nodded.

Chloe stood up from the chair and announced, "I hope you're all ready for dessert because I made a big chocolate cake."

All the children happily jumped up and started toward the table, deserting their toys on the hand-woven carpet.

Saul quickly spoke up. "Not so fast, *kinner*. Come put your toys away first, and then you can enjoy some chocolate cake." He then followed Chloe into the kitchen hoping to steal another kiss before the children joined them. As he spotted her removing dessert plates from the cupboard, he sneaked up behind her and wrapped his arms around her waist.

Chloe let out a laugh. "I'm surprised your arms even fit around me. My belly is so huge."

"It's not you that's big, it's the little one inside. I assume he'll be making his appearance before too long." He smiled, releasing her to her task. The kiss would have to come later.

Chloe sighed, and sat the dishes on the table. "*Jah*, I'm sure he will." She rubbed her lower back, trying to dissipate some of the pain.

"You all right, Chloe?" Saul eyed her with concern.

"*Jah*, I'm fine. Don't worry, the babe's not comin' yet." Her assuring smile seemed to melt the tenseness around his eyes.

All the children eagerly waited to be served as they clambered into the dining area and sat around the table. Chloe released the serving utensil to Saul's outstretched hand and he cut large slices for each of the children. She then returned to the kitchen for glasses and a jar of fresh goat milk from Danika. Each child and adult thoroughly enjoyed the chocolate cake, and then sat around the table chatting happily. When Nehemiah and Lyddie started dozing, Saul decided he'd better leave before it became too late for the *kinner*.

Chloe put the girls to bed, then escorted Saul and his children out to the buggy. After the children were settled into the buggy, Saul took Chloe by the hand and pulled her around the side of the vehicle out of the children's view. He pulled her into a warm embrace and attempted to kiss her, but she quickly stepped away. "*Nee*, Saul."

"Not even a good night kiss?" he pleaded.

"Just on the cheek, *jah*." Chloe allowed.

Saul pulled her close again and very slowly kissed her cheek, his lips lingering against her soft skin. "*Denki* for supper, Chloe. It was delicious," he whispered huskily.

"*Gern gheschen*," she answered after finding her voice. Why is it that she couldn't think clearly when Saul Brenneman was near? Perhaps it had something to do with the fact that she'd always found him so desirable. He released her from his embrace when he heard the children becoming restless. "You'd better go now," Chloe suggested.

Saul reluctantly climbed into his buggy and tipped his hat toward her, then disappeared down the lane.

SEVENTEEN

*S*aul inched a little closer to Chloe on the buggy seat and draped his arm around her shoulder. Being at Bella Italiano had rekindled special memories. As they neared the house after their delicious dinner date, Saul turned to Chloe. "I can't wait to meet Ruthie again."

"Yeah, she's excited about seeing you again too. I gotta warn you though, she speaks her mind." Chloe laughed.

"Just like I remember her. Hmm...I wonder where she gets *that* from," Saul teased as he opened the back door for Chloe. She walked into the kitchen and Saul followed close behind. Chloe was pleased to observe the kitchen neat and tidy and the house silent.

"Ruthie?" Chloe called quietly, not wanting to wake the girls in case they'd gone to bed already.

"I'm here, Chloe," she called in a hushed tone from the stairs. Ruthie descended the last step and smiled brightly when she spied Saul. "Saul Brenneman."

Saul walked over and briefly embraced her, and then held her at arm's length. "Would ya look at you? All grown up." He whistled low.

Ruthie smiled, stepped back, and then spun around with her arms out. "Almost seventeen." She giggled.

"Well, I bet you've got beaus lined up knocking on your door day and night," he teased. "Must be taking after your perty sister." He turned and winked at Chloe.

"Just one beau." Ruthie beamed. "Ethan Spencer."

"Spencer? I don't remember any Amish with the last name of Spencer." He raised his eyebrows. "You're not thinkin' of jumpin' the fence, are ya?"

"*Ach*, no. Ethan's not Amish...yet. But he's taking baptismal classes and instruction in the *Ordnung*." Her eyes shined.

"Oh?" Saul smiled knowingly. "And why would he be doing that?"

"We're gettin' married next fall!" Ruthie floated on cloud nine.

"Well, I should say he's a *schmeart* man to have caught you. Congratulations!" He reached over and patted her arm, and then took a seat on the couch next to Chloe.

"So, when are you and *mei schweschder* gettin' hitched?" Ruthie asked boldly, raising her eyebrows.

"*Ach*, Ruthie!" Chloe gasped, frowning at her sister.

Saul just chuckled. "You were right about that, Chloe. Ruthie is *definitely* not afraid to speak her mind." He glanced at

Ruthie, and then turned to Chloe and took her hand. "Actually, I was hoping to discuss that subject with your sister tonight."

Ruthie squealed with delight. "I knew it. I'll take that as my cue to go." Ruthie winked at her sister, who shook her head in disbelief at her audaciousness. Ruthie added as an afterthought, "As you probably already guessed, the girls are down for the night."

"*Denki*, Ruthie," Chloe called out to her sister before she waltzed out the back door.

Saul grinned broadly at Chloe. "Ruthie is somethin' else, isn't she? Hannah reminds me of her when she was younger."

"I've often thought that too. She'll be a handful, no doubt," Chloe said, and then glanced toward the kitchen. "Would you like something to drink, Saul?"

"Sure, but I'll get it. I'll get us both something. You stay off your feet." Saul kissed her forehead, and then got up and headed into the kitchen.

"There's some peppermint tea in the refrigerator," she called out. Chloe sighed, and then sent up a silent prayer. *Please, God. Show me how to approach this subject of salvation with Saul. I know it is important to you. Give me the words to say. Thy will be done, Lord.* Just as she said "Amen" Saul sauntered into the room with two glasses in hand.

"About what Ruthie mentioned earlier..." Saul set his tea down, speaking in a serious tone. "Chloe, I hope you'll say yes. Until I saw you at the store the other week, I thought that I would never marry again. I never had the desire to. From the very first day we met at that Singin', I knew we were meant to be together, that you were my soul mate. I'd never wanted to be with anyone else. I did learn to love Sarah, but when she and I were first married, I'm ashamed to say that I wished she was you. I kept hoping that it was all a bad dream and that I would wake up and you would be the one I had married. I know it was wrong to feel that way, but I couldn't help it. It took so long to get you out of my head, Chloe. But now...*ach*, I must sound like a rambling fool. What I mean to say is...will you marry me, Chloe?" His eyes were pleading.

Tears sprung to Chloe's eyes. What could she possibly say to that? "*Ach*, Saul. You're impossible not to love." She smiled.

"Is that a yes?" he asked anxiously.

"No. I mean, I don't know. I need some time." Sadness clenched her heart when Saul's hopeful countenance fell. "I mean, there are just things we need to discuss first."

Saul looked up. "What things?"

"Where we'd live. Which district. Things like that."

"I assumed you and the *kinner* would come and live with us," Saul said. "Are you opposed to that?"

"*Jah*, I am." Chloe released a sigh. "I'd like to stay here in Bishop Hostettler's district. We're New Order," she reminded him. "Our *Ordnung* is different. We believe the Bible teaches you can be saved and know it."

Saul mumbled something Chloe couldn't decipher. "I know. But I was hoping you would give up that foolishness." He blew out a breath.

She couldn't believe her ears. "Foolishness?! You think believing in God's Word is foolish, Saul Brenneman?" Chloe felt her voice raise an octave and struggled to temper her tone.

"I think going against the *Ordnung*, what our ancestors have always believed and taught, is foolish. It is prideful to proclaim you are saved."

"How can following God's Word and believing what it says be prideful?" she challenged.

Saul moved closer and gently rubbed Chloe's cheek with his fingers. He spoke softly, "Chloe, let's don't do this, *liewi*. I don't want to argue. Can't we just..." He leaned over and pressed his lips to hers. "...talk about this later, after we're married?"

Chloe moved away, trying her best not to let Saul persuade her with his sweet affections. "I see. So you want me to marry you and then we'll figure it all out. And then *you'll* be the head of the house and make all the decisions for *us*, right?"

"That's not what I'm trying to do." He blew out a breath.

"No?" Chloe skepticized. "*Ach*, Saul. Don't you see? This is too important not to discuss. If we marry, we have to be in agreement. I won't be unequally yoked."

"You make me sound like a heathen or something!" he said in exasperation. "I believe the same God you do, Chloe. Isn't that enough? Isn't our love for each other enough?"

"I'm sorry, Saul. But it is not." Chloe stared at her hands. "And I'm not going to change my mind about this."

Saul sighed and stood up, raking his hands through his hair. "I should probably go then. I can't think about this right now."

153

Unexpectedly, he leaned down and gave Chloe an exhilarating kiss, resulting in her knees weakening. "I love you, Chloe. But I...I can't do this again," his voice faltered as he spoke the words, and then he practically sprinted out the door.

The tears in the corners of Saul's eyes were almost Chloe's undoing. She wanted to run after him and tell him that, yes, she would marry him. She wanted to fall into his arms and never let him go. When would she see him again? *Would* she see him again? Did her chance for love and happiness just walk out the door?

She knew one thing for sure and for certain. She must seek God and ask Him to work on Saul's heart. That's all she could do, wasn't it? Yes, she would pray that God's will be done. After all, He's the one who sees the end from the beginning. He knows best. Chloe found comfort in knowing she could take her cares to God and lay them at His feet. The God of the universe was in control, and surely she could trust Him with her problems.

Just then, a voice from the past spoke. *Trust in the Lord with all thine heart; and lean not unto thine own understanding.* It was one of the last verses Levi had read from the Bible. Levi's words...God's words... hung in the air.

"I will, Lord," Chloe whispered, as a fresh wave of tears flooded her emerald eyes.

Saul's hands shook as he took up the horse's reins. *Not again. Why, Lord? Why can't I just have someone to love who lives by the* Ordnung? *Why is it that the only two women I've ever loved have to be deceived by this nonsense?*

He waited for an answer, but it never came.

Bishop Mast would never approve of his marriage to someone from Bishop Hostettler's district, unless they conformed to their *Ordnung.* That was their only hope for a life together. If he married Chloe in her district, he'd be shunned in his. Of course, Chloe's bishop would probably require him to conform to their district's teaching as well – something he was *not* willing to do. How could he embrace a teaching he didn't believe?

Saul thought back to the difficulties he and Sarah had experienced. Life had been terrible after she'd been shunned. In an attempt to bring her back into the flock, Saul was required to separate himself from his *fraa.* They weren't permitted to sleep in the same bedroom. They didn't eat together. He wasn't allowed to receive anything directly from her hands. No hugs, no kissing, no touching. All of these things were supposed to cause her to open her eyes.

But that never happened. Sarah had been steadfast in her beliefs and *nothing* was going to change that.

The *Bann* had taken a definite toll on their marriage. Finally, out of sheer desperation, Saul had said "Enough!" Three torturous years without his *fraa* next to him at night had been more than he could endure. He thought back to the day of his breaking point. *"I can't stand this any longer, Sarah. You are my* wife. *I* love *you*. *I* want *you*. *I* need *you*. Ordnung *or no, I'm not doing this anymore."* It had been one of the best and worst days of his life. So Saul voluntarily became shunned as well. He wished he'd done it sooner. If so, they'd certainly have a couple more *kinner* in addition to their four.

It hadn't taken long for Sarah's *vadder* to catch on. Pregnancy was a difficult thing to conceal. Saul hadn't been shunned outright. He gave a kneeling confession after the first time she was found with child. But when it was discovered that Sarah was in the family way again, a kneeling confession wouldn't do.

The years that Sarah had been shunned were gone forever. And now that she had passed from this world, Saul realized what a fool he'd been. He'd give anything to have those wasted years back. He knew now that it would have been better to choose to be shunned with Sarah from day one. How many precious moments had he lost with his beloved?

He'd been given a clean slate by the elders after Sarah died. Since he didn't believe as his wife had professed, and he'd confessed his transgression of refusing to shun Sarah, he was now no longer in the *Bann*. Although he didn't have his *fraa*, at least he could fellowship with his family now. All that would change if he married in a different district. Or if he married someone who believed as Sarah had.

With Chloe, though, it was different. It didn't *have* to be that way. He and Chloe could have a fresh start if she just changed her mind about this whole ridiculous thing. But it seemed Chloe was just as stubborn regarding this matter as Sarah was.

So he had two choices: marry the woman he loved and become shunned to the only family and community he'd ever known, or live alone as a single father and try to forget that he gave up, not one, but two of the most wonderful women that ever lived.

Both choices stunk.

EIGHTEEN

*C*hloe placed three of her best tea cups onto a tray with an assortment of herbal teas, and removed the kettle of water from the stove top. She walked into her living room and offered her two best friends, Joanna and Danika, and her sister, Ruthie, some refreshment. Her guests were a welcome distraction to her tumultuous thoughts of Saul. Balancing her trust in God with her conflicting emotions proved tremendously difficult.

Ruthie turned to Joanna. "So, what's it been like to marry an *Englischer* and becoming *Englisch*?"

Joanna shrugged. "Not much different. I mean, the *Englisch* world is different in a lot of ways, but I don't feel like I've changed that much. But I sure do miss you guys." Joanna laughed. "Oh no, I sound like you, Danika! We've switched places."

Danika smiled. "It's being in California, I'm sure. Caleb's folks live there, right?"

Joanna nodded, then frowned when she noticed Chloe's downtrodden countenance. "What's wrong, Chloe?"

"She's moping over Saul," Ruthie provided.

Joanna's brow raised. "Wait a minute. *Saul*? As in *'left you and broke your heart'* Saul?"

"That'd be the one," Ruthie answered. "Yep, Chloe *coincidentally* ran into the *widowed* Saul Brenneman at Walmart. They've already been courting." Ruthie's smile broadened.

"Ruthie," Chloe warned. "I can speak for myself."

"*Really?*" Joanna said with more than a hint of interest. She glanced at Danika and smiled. "And here I thought you were sad over Levi."

"She's been sad over Levi too. But this time it's Saul," Ruthie spoke.

"Ruthie!" Chloe huffed.

"So, let me get this straight. You and Saul Brenneman are *courting?*" Joanna said in disbelief.

"*Were* courting." Chloe rubbed her forehead. "Not anymore."

"Not yet," Ruthie interjected.

"Chloe and Saul are having a disagreement," Danika said. "You know, he's in Bishop Mast's district still. He's not saved."

"Oh." Joanna frowned.

"We've been praying for him, though." Danika offered Chloe an encouraging half-smile. "So we're not going to give up hope. Right, Chloe? God can move mountains with just a little bit of faith."

"God's will is best," Joanna said wisely.

Chloe nodded. "Yes, but my heart keeps telling me otherwise."

"Same ole problem, huh? We all experience that once in a while." Joanna touched Chloe's hand. "The last thing you want or need is to be married to someone that isn't saved. I've seen it so many times in the *Englisch* world. A lot of times, sadly, it ends in divorce. Just wait on God. His will *and* His timing are perfect."

"I'm doing my best, but it's hard not to think about it." Chloe frowned.

"So let's change the subject," Joanna said. She turned to Ruthie. "Jonathan said he wants to take Ethan hunting. Do you think he'll be up for it?"

Ruthie perked up. "Oh, *jah*! He's been talking about needing to learn to hunt. When does Jonathan want to go?"

"Before the snow falls," Joanna said.

"Okay, I'll tell him." Ruthie smiled, then jumped up when she heard her nieces awaking from their naps. "I'll get the girls."

Chloe looked at Joanna. "How long are you staying this time?"

"*Ach*, just till next week." Joanna frowned.

"When are you coming back?" Danika asked.

"Probably not until Christmas next year. Your *bopplin* will be walking by then, *jah*?" Joanna smiled. "Maybe Caleb and I will have another one too."

"Are you in the family way?" Chloe asked, placing a hand over the pain in her lower back.

"No. Just wishful thinking." Joanna eyed Chloe. "Are you alright?"

"*Jah*. Just a pain is all."

Danika sobered. "Are you sure?"

"I still have five weeks left," Chloe assured. She grimaced when another pain surfaced.

"Chloe?" Joanna asked unconvinced.

"I'm sure it's nothing." Chloe waved a hand in front of her face as though swatting a fly, and tried to ignore the next dull pain. She brightened when Ruthie entered the room with Hannah and Lydia.

NINETEEN

*C*hloe's absence from his life was driving Saul mad. He had hoped that if he left her alone for a couple weeks, perhaps she would come running back to him. But she hadn't. In fact, he hadn't heard a word from her. Was she moving on without him? The thought was unsettling. Now that he'd become reacquainted with Chloe and their love had been rekindled, he couldn't imagine living the rest of his life without her. She invaded his thoughts daily.

Nothing was the same. He'd been quick tempered with the children. He couldn't focus on his projects at work and constantly had to redo things. There was a rift between him and his *Englisch* neighbor. In truth, he felt his life was falling apart.

He thought of Sarah and Chloe. How could two women hold on to the same thing so fiercely? Why was this so important to them? Why couldn't they let it go – not even for his love? Was there anything more important than the love between a man and a woman? He'd asked himself the same questions, pondering his own answers. Had he been wrong?

"Okay, Lord. What do You want from me?" He threw up his hands in desperation. "I've only followed what I've always been taught. I thought I was supposed to honor my father and mother. Aren't we supposed to keep the faith of our fathers? Not follow some new gospel. I don't understand." The words hung like stale air in the expanse of his work shop where he sat all alone. He placed his head in his hands. "I need answers, Lord."

No audible voice sounded, but a stream of light filtering through a crack in the wall caught his eye. It seemed to illuminate a specific corner of the barn. Sarah's cedar box.

He strode over to his *fraa's* old hope chest. Aside from moving it out of their bedroom, he'd left it untouched since she'd gone. One day, he'd planned on giving it to Amanda Chloe, perhaps as a wedding gift. He lifted the tarp and blanket that covered the chest and opened the cedar lid.

He anxiously examined the contents, as bittersweet memories of his and Sarah's life together flooded his thoughts. He reached for Sarah's worn Bible. As he opened the cover, an envelope slipped out and fell to the dirt floor near his boot. He picked it up and brushed the dirt off. When he turned it over, he noticed his name. Saul hastily opened the envelope and pulled out a piece of folded lined paper. He swallowed a lump in his throat when he unfolded the letter. The strip of photos of him and Chloe, that he'd thrown away years ago, were tucked safely inside. *Where...?*

Saul glanced down at Sarah's handwriting. He read his *fraa's* words in dismay...

Dear Saul,

Thank you for being a good husband to me and a good father to our children. I love you.

If you're reading this note, it means that I'm now in Heaven with Jesus. I knew this day would come. When I first became sick, I knew God had answered my prayer. You see, I've been praying for you for years. With all my heart, I desired to share God's love with you but you would never allow it. So I prayed that if my leaving your world would open your eyes to His Truth, that God would take me home.

My guess is that God is working on your heart right now. Please listen to Him. Please look at the verses I marked in this Bible.

Love,

Sarah

P.S. I don't know why I kept the pictures of you and your former aldi. I guess I just hated to see them thrown away. She'd meant so much to you at one time. Perhaps God has something else planned for you now that I'm gone?

After wiping a lone tear from his cheek, he haphazardly opened Sarah's Bible. Looking down, he read the words from Proverbs chapter three. *Trust in the Lord with all thine heart; and lean not unto thine own understanding.*

He paused.

"Is that what I'm doing, Lord? Leaning on my own understanding? Am I not trusting You enough?" He continued reading, *In all thy ways acknowledge him, and he shall direct thy paths.*

"Direct my paths, Lord. Show me what to do," he called out.

"*Dat? Dat?*" Amanda Chloe hollered from the barn door, jarring Saul from his rumination. "Aren't you going to answer the telephone? I've heard it ring ten times now!"

Deep in thought, Saul had been oblivious to the noisy device. He heard it loud and clear now, though. He stared at it blankly.

Amanda Chloe gasped. "Well, do you want me to get it?"

"Sure." He shrugged.

"Hello?" she sang out into the receiver. "*Jah, Dat's* right here. May I ask who's calling?" Amanda Chloe turned to Saul and shrugged. "She says her name is Ruthie."

Saul jumped up and frantically grabbed the phone from her hand. "Ruthie? What is it? Is something wrong?" His heart beat a hundred miles per hour as he waited for her response.

"Early? Which hospital is she in? Okay, Ruthie. I'll get there as quickly as I can." He abruptly hung up the receiver and turned to Amanda Chloe. "I need you to go pack some clothes for yourself and the boys. I'm going to drop you off at *Mammi's*. Chloe needs me now. Be quick about it." Amanda Chloe turned on her heel and sped to the house, while Saul picked up the telephone to call a hired driver.

Saul inwardly cringed when he stepped out of the elevator and saw Bishop Hostettler standing in the waiting room. What all had the man heard of him and his shaded past? He was well aware that the local bishops kept in contact, despite their doctrinal differences. What must he think of him? Certainly not as a formidable mate for his widowed daughter-in-law. He sighed. His steps grew heavier as he neared the cluster of Plain folk.

"Saul, thank God you're here!" a sunny voice rang out from behind him. He turned around to see Ruthie's pleased countenance. "Come with me."

Before he could respond, Ruthie clutched his arm and led him down a seemingly unending corridor. He followed along like a blind puppy on a leash. They turned the corner and Ruthie opened a door with a number on it. "Wait here. I'll be right back." Ruthie disappeared into the room.

Saul clenched his hands together wondering what Ruthie was thinking bringing him to the room where her sister was about to give birth. He ran a hand through his hair, contemplating whether he should turn around and bolt back to the waiting room. Ruthie pushed through the door once again with her mother and Danika Yoder in tow. They were obviously surprised to see him.

"Just a few minutes, please. Her contractions are getting closer," Danika said, who appeared close to birth herself.

"I...I can wait." He hesitated.

"Don't be silly, Saul." Ruthie pushed him from behind. "Just go see her."

Reluctantly, Saul swung the door open and padded inside. Thankfully, the first bed was empty. A large curtain veiled the bed in which Chloe lay and he took a deep breath before stepping near. He slowly walked toward the bed where Chloe reclined clad in a white and blue hospital gown, her *kapp* slightly askew. The look of shock on her face told him that she was not expecting him.

"Saul?" Her eyes widened. "What are you doing here?" She self-consciously pulled her gown closer to her neck.

"Uh, well, I, uh...Ruthie called me," he managed. *Oh, why did I even come?*

Chloe's face turned sober and she began panting. Saul rushed to her bedside and grasped her hand. "Are you all right? Is there something I can do for you?" She squeezed his hand tightly, unable to speak. Saul waited in silence, unsure of what to do. He'd never been present at any of Sarah's births.

A short while later, Chloe took a deep breath and spoke, "*Denki* for coming, Saul." She smiled in appreciation. "Oh, no." She began frantically panting again and squeezed his hand so hard he was sure it was no match for man's strength. She groaned. "The baby! I need to push!"

"I'll get your *mamm*," Saul said.

Chloe reluctantly released his hand. He ran to the door and summoned a nearby nurse. To his dismay, neither Chloe's mother, nor Danika, nor Ruthie were anywhere in sight. He looked both ways down the hall and glanced over to the nurses' station, noticing the nurse on duty hadn't gone into Chloe's room yet.

He couldn't leave Chloe in there alone. Making a snap decision, he rushed back into the delivery room.

"My *mamm*?" Chloe asked desperately.

Saul gave her a hopeless look and shook his head. "I'll stay as long as you want me to," he attempted reassurance.

A different nurse than the one at the station entered the room, she brightened at the sight of Saul. "Oh, good! Daddy showed up. Looks like this little one will be here before we know it." The nurse glanced at Saul's anxious expression and patted his shoulder. "Don't worry about a thing, your wife will be just fine. Now, go over there and hold her hand and give her the encouragement she needs. Just don't go passing out on me."

Saul looked at Chloe helplessly, and she gave him an encouraging half-smile before her face contorted. "Saul! Help." He rushed to her side once again and crouched down next to her bed. He slipped one arm around her back and held her hand with the other one.

"You can do this, Chloe. *Der Herr* is with you," he encouraged.

"I need to push!" Chloe cried.

"Go ahead, honey," the nurse recommended.

Chloe bore down and grasped Saul's hand with one hand and the bed rail with the other. She closed her eyes and pushed with all her might. Perspiration dripped from her forehead. "Ugh!" She leaned back on the bed, exhausted.

"You're doing great, honey. Looks like this one has dark hair," the nurse observed from the other end of the bed, and then asked Saul to push the red button on the bed.

"Again!" Chloe leaned forward and pushed, thankful for Saul's comforting presence.

"Okay, the head is out. I just need to make sure the cord isn't wrapped around the baby's neck before you push again." The nurse glanced toward the door in expectation and in rushed a female doctor and another nurse pushing a transparent plastic bassinet. The doctor quickly pulled a pair of latex gloves over her hands.

"It's coming, I can't stop it!" Chloe called out.

"I'll take over from here," the doctor said, and then questioned the previous attendant. "All clear?"

"Yes, Doctor. She's ready to go," the nurse confirmed as she moved aside.

Saul watched as the other attendants began gathering and preparing items needed for after the delivery.

The doctor looked to Chloe, who seemed to be holding back. "Okay, go for it."

Saul whispered in Chloe's ear, and lovingly kissed her cheek. With renewed confidence, she asked for Divine strength and pushed again. A tear trickled down her flustered cheek when she heard a small cry and the doctor announced, "Congratulations, you have a baby boy!"

"Levi," she whispered, as more tears pricked the corners of her eyes then flowed freely. *You have a son, Levi.*

TWENTY

*S*tephen Esh glanced out the side window of his home when he heard a buggy roll to a stop. He scowled when he realized Saul Brenneman stood on the back porch of his residence. It'd been many years since he'd seen Saul, but not enough in Stephen's opinion.

Last he saw of Saul, his sister was in tears for weeks. They'd been courting for a while and were engaged to be married. Shortly thereafter, Stephen had heard that Saul married another woman. One that was expecting *his* child. What kind of a jerk would do that to a teenage girl? Fortunately, his good friend Levi, an *honorable* Amish man, had come along to help heal Chloe's broken heart.

Stephen grudgingly opened the door.

"Hey, Stephen." Saul reached out his hand, smiling broadly. "It's been awhile."

Reluctantly, Stephen took Saul's hand and purposely shook it a bit too firmly, clearly demonstrating his physical advantage. "*Jah*, you could say that," he said wryly.

Saul's smile quickly faded and he shifted from one foot to the other. Stephen made no bones about *not* being happy to see him. Saul would do well to get to the point quickly. "Did you get the message from Ruthie?"

"I did," he stated. He stood with his arms crossed over his chest, blocking the back entrance into the kitchen. Stephen was a year younger than Saul, but towered over him by six inches. His broad shoulders and thick forearms indicated he could probably knock Saul down with one swift blow, if he had a mind to.

Saul realized he'd better get on with his business before he irritated Stephen any longer. He was no wimp, and definitely not one to back down from a challenge, but he didn't wish to put more rift between Chloe and himself.

Stephen clearly was not going to make this easy. Saul hadn't been prepared for a confrontation with Chloe's older brother, but apparently it was inevitable. Perhaps the humble approach would be best. "Listen, Stephen. I'm sorry for what happened in the past. I never intended to hurt your sister, you must know that. I–"

"Save your breath, Brenneman. Just do what you came here for." Stephen glowered, slightly moving out of the way for Saul to pass.

Saul nodded, barely squeezed past him, and stepped into the dining area of Chloe's childhood home. Fond memories came flooding back like a burst of sunshine topping the east-ern mountains in the early morning. He closed his eyes, mo-mentarily soaking in the healing rays. This was where he'd first met Chloe's beloved family, so full of love and energy. It's where he'd decided he wanted to become a permanent part of that familial structure. But that love was starkly contrasted with the cold, even hostile greeting he'd received from Stephen. A burned bridge badly in need of repair.

He sighed heavily, and then quickly brightened when little Hannah entered the room. "Hannah! It's *gut* to see you." Saul stretched his arms for a hug, but instead of running into his embrace, the young girl stood defiant like a statue, her bottom lip protruding. He dropped his arms to his sides and cocked his head. "What's wrong, Hannah?"

"You went away. You weft us wike *Dat* did." Her small chin began to quiver. "I fought you went to Heaben to wib wif Jesus."

Saul glanced at the doorway only to catch Stephen's glare. "I swear, Saul." He breathed out. "If you hurt Chloe's *kinner–*"

Saul abruptly held up his hand. "I won't." He scowled. "Let's save this discussion for another time." His eyes gestured toward Hannah, and Stephen nodded curtly in agreement.

Saul stepped forward, crouched down next to Hannah, and stroked her arm reassuringly. "Don't cry, *liewi.*"

Hannah lifted her big hazel eyes to his. "*Mamm* said you didn't go da Heaben. I can't wait to go da Heaben and see my fiwst *Dat*. I can go thewe now 'cause Jesus took my sins away. I don't gots no sins no more." She shook her head for emphasis.

Saul smiled at Chloe's precious daughter.

"Do you still got sins, *Dat*?" Hannah asked wide-eyed, looking into Saul's kind face.

"Do not call *him Dat*." Stephen's ire rose. "Saul is *not* your *vadder*, Hannah!"

"*Jah, Onkel* Steben! He was kissin' *Mamm* on the wips. *Mamm* onwy kisses *Dat* on the wips, ain't so?" Hannah adamantly protested.

Saul noticed Stephen clenching his fists. It was clear he had heard about all he could take. "Enough, Hannah!" Stephen's voice shook the room and Hannah ran into Saul's arms.

Oh boy, I'd better leave quickly.

Stephen's mind whirled. *Saul and Chloe kissing? And in front of the* kinner? *This guy has more nerve than I gave him credit for. Unbelievable!*

Back when Chloe and Saul were courting, Stephen knew his sister had been too careless with Saul. Too intimate. She'd even come home with a "monkey bite" one time, as their younger sister Ruthie called it.

But he knew for a fact that Chloe and Levi had stayed completely pure during their entire six year courtship with nary a kiss on the cheek. Now, with Levi barely gone six months, Saul swept in like a vulture to no doubt take advantage of his sister once again. He had to protect her. Or at least talk some sense into his *ferhoodled* sister. All he knew is that this man needed to leave his house before he did something he'd regret.

"We're leaving now. Where's Lyddie?" Saul glanced around the room.

"Yes. You'd better leave," Stephen threatened. "She's upstairs with my *kinner*. I'll bring her out," Stephen hissed, and then sharply turned toward the stairs with purposeful steps.

After Stephen escorted young Lydia outside, he watched to be certain sure Saul's hired driver found his way off his property. The sooner Saul and the girls left his place, the better for all of them.

Saul held Lyddie in one arm and Hannah with the other as they peered through the glass at the hospital nursery. He surveyed the many plexiglass bassinets that held babies of all colors, shapes, and sizes, in search of little Levi. He spotted the infant in an incubator several feet away. "Do you see your brother? He's in there." He pointed to the large cream colored box with clear sides and two round windows.

"I can't see 'im, *Dat*. He's too faw away," Hannah protested, squinting her eyes to try to get a better view. "Why's he in dat box aw by 'imsewf?"

"That box is called an incubator. That's where they sometimes put babies that are very small. It helps them to get bigger and stronger. Your brother Levi was premature. That means he was born too early," Saul informed the young girls, not certain how much they actually comprehended.

"He's awfwy witto, ain't so? I wanna see 'im betto," she whined.

"Yes, Hannah, he's awfully little." Saul motioned to one of the neonatal nurses, asking her to roll the incubator closer to the glass. The nurse, clad with latex gloves and a paper face mask, nodded her reply and wheeled the large contraption closer so they could see the tiny dark haired boy. Prior to Levi's birth, he had never seen an Amish baby so small. The babe could probably fit in the palm of his large hand.

Hannah gasped when she gazed on her baby brother. "Wook, *Dat*. Webi has a big white bag on 'im."

Saul chuckled. "That's a diaper, Hannah. It just looks big because Levi is so little."

"*Boppi!*" Lyddie spoke up, her lips turned up in a grin.

"That's right, Lyddie. That's a *boppli, dein bruder*," he said.

"I wanna howd 'im. Can we take 'im home today, *Dat*?" Hannah asked, watching her brother yawn and stretch out his tiny arms and legs.

"Probably not today. We'll have to talk to the doctor and see when he can come home. Hopefully, Levi won't need to be here too much longer."

"What's dat fing on 'is awm?" Hannah stared at the wristband and wondered aloud.

"That's so they know the baby belongs to your *mamm* and not someone else. Your mother has a wristband on, too. They both have the same numbers on them. Since there's a lot of babies here, they don't want to get them mixed up," Saul said.

"Oh...Can we go back and see *Mamm* now? I miss 'er."

"Me, too. Sure, let's go find her room." Saul set the two girls down and led them by the hand down the hallway.

TWENTY-ONE

*T*he sight of Saul walking into the room, hand in hand with her daughters, made Chloe's heart melt. Oh, if only they could work out their differences. Even at Chloe's chiding, Hannah insisted on calling Saul *"Dat"*. She simply wouldn't believe otherwise. What would happen if their relationship was never restored? She couldn't bear for little Hannah to get her heart broken again. She'd already lost her real father and that had been difficult enough.

Why was Saul here, anyway? Did he have a change of heart? Was he willing to talk and search through the scriptures now? Or did he just come because he thought she was in some kind of trouble? If it was the latter, then it would be best if he went on his way as quickly as possible. The less time he spent with her and the girls, the fewer pieces she would have to pick up and glue back together later.

"*Mamm, Mamm*! *Dat* took us to see Webi!" Hannah beamed, moving to her mother's side. "He's so cute and witto. But *Dat* says we can't take 'im home yet."

"Hannah, Saul is not *Dat*," Chloe said adamantly. She needed to lay this to rest once and for all.

"Uh, huh!" Hannah insisted, and then ran back to Saul, grabbing his hand possessively. Clearly, she desired a father. No, she needed a father.

Chloe looked to Saul with pleading eyes. Saul then spoke up, "Hannah, what your *mamm* says is true. I'm not your *da–*"

Her eyes filled with tears. She spoke with a shaky voice, "*Jah*, you are. You kissed *Mamm* on the wips! I saw y–"

Saul placed a finger over her lips before she could finish. He knelt down and came face to face with the young girl, gently stroking her small hand and speaking softly, "Hannah, I want you to listen to me. Will you do that?" The girl nodded. "I know I kissed your *mamm*. Perhaps I shouldn't have done that because we aren't married. Not yet." He glanced up at Chloe with hopeful eyes. "If it's God's will, then maybe someday we will be married and I will become your *dat*. But until then, you can't say that I am your *dat* because that would be lying. You don't want to lie, do you?"

"Wying is a sin, ain't so?" Hannah asked wide-eyed.

"That's right," Saul answered.

"But I don't gots no sins. *Mamm* said Jesus watched aw my sins away. Ain't so, *Mamm*?" Hannah asked.

Chloe nodded affirmatively. "That's right, Hannah. Jesus washed all your sins away when you trusted Him to save you. That's called grace. But you should never sin on purpose, God forbids us to. Do you understand?" She glanced up at Saul to gauge his reaction to her words. He seemed to be listening intently and for that, Chloe was thankful.

"And I gots a fancy home in Heaben, too. *Jah?*"

"That's what God promised us, Hannah," her mother confirmed.

"And *Gott* neber wies. Ain't so, *Mamm?*" Hannah looked to her mother again for reaffirmation.

Chloe nodded. "Yes, Hannah, God never lies. Jesus said, 'I am the way, the truth, and the life. No man cometh unto the Father but by me.' He cannot lie because He is Truth." She sent up a silent prayer for Saul who appeared to be in deep thought. Chloe wondered what he was thinking, but didn't dare ask.

Chloe felt Saul's eyes intent on hers and glanced his way. Unable to read his expression, she lifted her eyebrows in question. He nodded toward the children indicating he wished to speak with her alone. Their silent communication continued as she shrugged her shoulders. Since they were the only adults present at the moment, their conversation would have to wait for another time. Three loud knocks drew their attention to the door.

Saul sauntered to the room's entrance, opening the door wide for Danika and Ruthie. "*Wilkom!*"

"*Denki*, Saul. I hope we're not interrupting." Danika looked to Chloe for confirmation, spying Hannah and Lyddie nearby.

"*Nee.* But would you mind taking the girls down to the cafeteria for a bit? They could use a snack and some water," Chloe said with pleading eyes.

"Of course. Girls, let's go get a snack and maybe we'll go by and see Levi again." Danika understood Chloe's silent message that she and Saul wished to be alone, and she obliged. The girls' eyes sparkled at the mention of their baby brother.

Saul dug into his pocket and thrust a twenty dollar bill into Danika's hand. "Use it for the girls." He turned to Chloe, raising an eyebrow. "Would you like something, Chloe?"

Chloe shook her head. "No, *denki*."

After the door closed, Saul and Chloe were left alone. Saul appeared to be deep in contemplation when he took a seat at Chloe's bedside, cracking his knuckles. He abruptly stood up and began pacing to and fro on the tile floor near the foot of the hospital bed, reminding Chloe of a foot soldier. Chloe silently communed with the Lord, waiting patiently until Saul was ready to speak.

"So, let me get this straight. You told Hannah that she *is* going to Heaven for certain? Why would you tell her that?" Saul asked incredulously.

Chloe blew out her hopeful breath, dreading another argument with Saul. "She is. That's what God's Word teaches. 'For whosoever shall call upon the name of the Lord shall be saved,'" she recited the verse from memory.

"Something from the forbidden Scriptures." He huffed.

"No, not forbidden. Not to us. Don't you see, Saul? The reason Martin Luther translated the Bible into the German language is so the common people could have the Scriptures and read them for themselves," Chloe reasoned. "Don't you think

God *wants* us to have His *complete* Word and not just what someone *allows* us to read? The bishop and ministerial brethren may be our leaders, but they are not God. No more than the religious leaders were in Martin Luther's day."

Saul remained silent, seemingly chewing on her words.

Chloe rummaged through her bag that sat next to the bed on the floor. She pulled out a small black Bible and turned to the book of Second Timothy. She pointed to verse sixteen of chapter three and handed it to Saul. "Please read this."

Saul reluctantly took the Bible from her hands. "It's in English?"

"Yes. We're allowed to read the Scriptures in English," Chloe confirmed. "It is the King James Version, and has been trusted by Christians for hundreds of years."

He stared down at the book in his hands, and then finally read the verse aloud, "All scripture is given by inspiration of God, and is profitable for doctrine, for reproof, for correction, for instruction in righteousness..." he continued reading the next verse silently. He couldn't pull his eyes away as he read the verses over and over, absorbing their meaning.

"Will you please consider talking to Bishop Hostettler? I know that he can explain it all better than I can." Her eyes pleaded with his. She sensed an internal battle waging in Saul's mind and prayed the truth would win out.

"Did you know that my *fraa* was shunned for believing this?"

"No, I didn't. Many have gone through much worse than the *Bann*." Chloe noticed a faint misting in Saul's eyes. "So, Sarah was saved?"

"She said so."

"That's *wunderbaar*." Chloe smiled.

She waited for what seemed like an eternity for Saul to speak. He released a breath he'd been holding a little too long and had to grasp the bed rail to regain his bearings. "I don't need to speak with Bishop Hostettler, Chloe. I've made a decision."

Now Chloe was the one holding her breath. She couldn't read his complex expression. Oh, how she hated being kept in suspense. She couldn't stand it any longer. "And?"

"I had been praying, asking God for answers, when Ruthie called to tell me about you. I was a little confused at first, but now I understand. Chloe, He's never given me a clearer answer. I *know* what God wants me to do, I'm certain of it." Saul gave her the sweetest smile she'd ever seen. "I've decided to become a member of Bishop Hostettler's New Order district."

"Does this mean that you believe, that you've decided to trust Christ?" She wanted to be sure she understood correctly.

"Yes, that is what it means." His smile broadened.

"Oh, Saul! I couldn't think of better news." She felt like hopping out of her hospital bed and jumping for joy. Her countenance quickly sobered. "But, won't you be shunned?"

Saul nodded. "It's not going to be easy. But God wants me to trust Him. Before I came to see you, I read a verse from

Sarah's Bible. It was about trusting God with all my heart. I can't remember exactly how it goes."

"Trust in the Lord with all thine heart and lean not unto thine own understanding. In all thy ways, acknowledge him and he shall direct thy paths." Chloe quoted the verse that had kept her afloat during her trying times.

"Yes, that's it."

Chloe shook her head in wonder. "That was one of the last verses Levi read to me before he died. It has given me strength to carry on."

"That's amazing." Saul's eyes locked with Chloe's and silence reigned briefly. Saul took Chloe's hand in his. "Chloe Hostettler, *now*, will you please marry me?"

Chloe nodded and tears pricked her eyes.

"Wunderbaar!"

"But you'll still have to talk to the bishop."

"I know."

"And we'll have to wait until the mourning period is over," she reminded.

"I know."

"And we'll have to–"

"Chloe, will you shut up and kiss me?"

"Well, I nev–" her voice cut off when Saul's lips met hers. Chloe closed her eyes, allowing herself to momentarily delight in her betrothed's delicious attentions. If nothing else, Saul Brenneman knew how to kiss.

You shouldn't be doing this, a voice inside her head reminded. She suddenly recalled the words of her beloved Levi prior to their marriage, and guilt flooded her soul. *"I won't take kisses from you because they're not mine; they belong to your husband."* Levi had always been so good, so pure. She'd always had a hard time resisting temptation when Saul was near, so she silently pled for help from the Lord.

Before she succeeded unlocking their lips, the door behind them swung open. Saul jumped back sending the small table behind him crashing to the floor. The toppled pitcher of water ran under Chloe's bed while the plastic cup rocked back and forth then came to an eventual stop. Saul's and Chloe's mortified countenances told all.

"I see you got caught with your hand in the cookie jar again." Danika chuckled.

Hannah, Lyddie, and Ruthie all looked on in disbelief at the disaster on the floor. Saul hurriedly knelt down to wipe up the mess when Chloe clasped his arm to stop him.

"We have an announcement to make," Chloe declared excitedly. "For your ears only, of course."

"Ach, jah." Saul stood erect and cleared his throat, and then scanned each of the faces in the room. His gaze stopped on Hannah and Lyddie, anticipating their response. "Girls, how would you feel if I became your new *vadder*?"

The young girls stood wide-eyed, then a slow smile crept across Hannah's face.

Saul explained, "Your *mamm* and I have decided to get married!"

Hannah ran to Saul and threw her arms around his legs. "I knowed you was 'posed to be my *dat*! I pwayed and *Gott* said yes." Saul reached down and picked her up, placing a prickly kiss on her cheek. Hannah giggled. "That tickoes."

They weren't sure whether Lydia understood or not until her gaze darted from Chloe to Saul and she spoke softly, *"Dat?"* Her eyes were wide with expectation.

"Yes, Lyddie. Saul will be your *dat* soon," Chloe confirmed.

Saul knelt down next to the small girl and held out his arms. She walked into them, squeezing his neck tightly, and he scooped her up into the air. Surprisingly, she leaned close to Saul and kissed his cheek, giving him an adorable smile to boot. Lyddie then reached for Chloe and Saul handed the child to her mother.

"I knew it. Congratulations!" Ruthie smiled, offering a hug to both Chloe and Saul. "Does this mean you'll be getting married before Ethan and me?"

"Denki," Chloe said, returning her sister's embrace. "I'm not sure. We still need to speak with Bishop Hostettler."

"Uh oh. I don't fink *Onkel* Steben is gonna be happy," Hannah interjected, shaking her head with a worried expression. "He don't want Saul to be mine and Wyddie's *Dat*. He don't wike 'im."

Chloe sent Saul an inquisitive look and he shrugged his shoulders.

"Your *mamm* and I can discuss that later," Saul suggested. "You don't need to worry about it, Hannah."

Chloe nodded, wondering just what had transpired between Saul and Stephen.

TWENTY-TWO

Chloe held precious little Levi in her arms and wept over the realization that he would never know his real father. When she'd first learned of the new life growing inside her, she never dreamed she'd be raising him without Levi. Although Saul was now in her life, her heart still ached for her beloved Levi at times. But God's will had been done and there was nothing that could bring Levi back. She must be thankful for the five wonderful years God had given them together as husband and wife and the three children He'd blessed them with.

She hoped Saul would make a good step-father for her children and prayed that combining their two families would not present any problems. She'd heard of other families that had combined in the same way and the results had been disastrous. Fortunately, their children were still young so perhaps the transition would go smoothly.

Since she hadn't spent much time with Saul's *kinner*, she wasn't sure how they felt about her presence in their lives. With her pregnancy, the rocky relationship with Saul, and the *boppli* recently home, she hadn't had much extra time. She decided a picnic would be a good way for the two families to become better acquainted. Saul was excited when she suggested picnicking at Millers' pond, eager to take the older boys fishing. Chloe thought it would present a good opportunity for her and Amanda Chloe to get to know each other better.

With Levi's feeding complete, the baby now slept soundly. Chloe deposited the babe in his cradle, one that Levi had crafted before Hannah was born, and tiptoed out of her bedroom. Now she could begin preparing for their outing.

"Whatcha doin', *Mamm*?" Hannah's voice called from the kitchen entrance. She'd been told to play with Lydia in the living room.

"Just makin' the lunch for our picnic today," Chloe answered.

"I wanna hewp!" Hannah eagerly skipped to Chloe's side near the counter.

"I don't know about that. Did you clean up your things in the living room?"

Hannah shook her head. "Wyddie's still pwayin' wif 'em."

"If you want to help me, go put the toys away and bring Lyddie in here with you. Be quiet though, because your baby *bruder* is sleeping," Chloe warned.

"*Mamm*, I wub Webi," Hannah said.

"I know you do, *liewi*. Levi is precious to all of us," Chloe stated.

"Eben to *Dat*?"

"Now, which *daed* are you talking about this time? Do you mean Levi or Saul?"

"Webi, my fiwst *Dat*." Her expression was somber.

"Levi is especially precious to *Dat*. And to God. Now go do what I told you to do. Saul and the *kinner* will be here soon." Chloe shooed Hannah off, took a deep breath, and swiped the tears from her cheeks. Losing Levi had certainly been the most difficult trial she'd ever experienced.

Chloe lifted her eyes when she noticed Saul approaching the picnic blanket. "What are you doing back already? I thought you wanted to fish with the boys."

Saul laughed. "That lasted a whole ten minutes. The boys decided skipping rocks was much more fun than waiting to catch a fish." He shrugged. "I guess they're still a bit young for fishing. Besides, I don't mind spending time with my *aldi*."

"It seems like the *kinner* are getting along well." Chloe looked to where the older children now played tag near the opposite shore. Lyddie and Levi slept on the quilt next to her, and Nehemiah appeared to be leaning in that direction.

"*Jah*. How's this one been?" Saul ruffled his youngest son's hair and the two-year-old giggled.

"*Gut*. Although he got awfully curious when I was feeding Levi." Chloe laughed. "He thought the *boppli* was playing peek-a-boo."

"This one does tend to get a little curious, and out of hand, once in a while. I guess that's from lack of a *mamm* to help raise him. I'm afraid I'm not a very *gut* mother." He frowned.

Chloe smiled. "I wouldn't think so. But I'm sure you're a wonderful *vadder*."

"I try my best, but I'm lacking terribly in some areas."

"Tell me about your *fraa*."

Saul's brow lifted. "You want to know about Sarah?"

"*Jah*." Chloe nodded. "What was she like? How did you two get along?"

"I would think that after I left you, you'd never want to hear about her again."

"Well, I admit that might have been true when I first found out. I mean, I was heartbroken. I think the only time I've ever cried more was when my Levi died." She pushed a lone strand of hair off her cheek. "Of course, I was only fourteen when we were courting so I'm quite certain part of my anguish was due to immaturity. Not that I didn't love you and feel that my world was completely crumbling. It was all just such a shock at the time."

"I know what you mean. I was pretty messed up myself. I was still in love with you when Sarah and I married." Saul sighed. "Sarah and I had a pretty rough road at first. I blamed her for being pregnant; I'd thought she'd done it on purpose." He shook his head. "Talk about immaturity."

"So, what happened?"

"I'm afraid I hurt her pretty bad – not physically speaking, but emotionally. I said some pretty nasty things to her. But Sarah wasn't afraid to speak her mind. She made it quite clear that *I* wasn't exactly what she had planned either. *That* was like a slap in the face. I was certainly *hochmut*, but she put me in my place. Of course, we had some help from my folks." Saul loosely grasped Chloe's hand. "I'm sorry, I must sound like I'm babbling to you."

"*Nee.* I understand." Chloe squeezed his hand reassuringly. "But it does wonder me why you don't have more *kinner*. Did it take that long for you and Sarah to forgive each other?"

Saul chuckled. "No, we actually mended pretty fast." He quickly sobered and released another sigh, then continued. "Remember I told you that Sarah had gotten shunned? She was put in the *Bann* shortly after Amanda Chloe was born, so we didn't have much, or any, I should say, physical contact."

"How did her shunning come about?"

"She had gotten saved and tried to witness to her father, Bishop Mast. It didn't go well." He grimaced.

"Oh, Saul. I'm sorry." She glanced down at Saul's youngest, who appeared to be dozing off next to Lyddie. "But you had more *kinner*. Did her father lift the *Bann*?"

"*Nee.* I became shunned too. I loved her and couldn't stand to be without her. I hated what the Bann was doing to our marriage."

"So, you are shunned now?"

193

"No. Not yet, anyway. But as soon as I tell Bishop Mast that I plan to marry in another district, all that will change." He sighed and continued. "After Sarah died, I 'repented' so that I could be accepted back into the fold. Since I wasn't a believer, like my *fraa* had been, they had no qualms about taking me back. I could do without my folks and my siblings while I had Sarah, but after she died I realized that I needed them. There was no way I could raise these little ones alone." He rubbed young Nehemiah's back. "Being in the *Bann* was hard. I could no longer work with my *vadder*, so I had to start my own business from scratch. None of our People would do business with me, so I had to rely on *Englischers*. Our income dropped considerably and we nearly lost the house I'd built for us. Fortunately, my folks lent us some money – without the leaders knowing, of course."

Chloe shook her head. "I'm sorry you and Sarah had such a difficult time. How did she die?"

"Pneumonia. It happened quickly." Saul rubbed his forehead. "But I really think she died because of me."

"*You?*"

"She asked God to do whatever it took to get me to open my eyes to His Truth. Even if it meant taking her out of this world. She knew God answered her prayer when she got sick. Sarah was content, though. She knew she was going to die, but she died having faith that God's love would reach my heart." He reached over and rubbed Chloe's arm and smiled. "And it has, thanks to you."

"She was a remarkable woman."

"Yes. And so are you." Saul leaned close and gently caressed Chloe's cheek.

Chloe was a little disappointed that she didn't get much time with Amanda Chloe today. Not that she minded spending time with Saul; no, in fact, she enjoyed his presence immensely. But she'd hoped that she could get Amanda Chloe to open up to her and share her feelings. She not only wanted to be Amanda Chloe's step-mother after she and Saul married, but also her mentor and friend.

As she put the picnic items away, Saul and his *kinner* entered the kitchen. "Well, it looks like the buggy's all cleaned out. The *kinner* did a *gut* job." Saul smiled.

Amanda Chloe's cheeks seemed a little pink and Chloe wondered if maybe she had been exposed to a tad too much sunshine.

Saul nudged his daughter. "Go ahead. Ask her."

Chloe's curiosity piqued. "Ask me what?"

Amanda Chloe hesitantly spoke up. "*Dat* said that you like to ride horses. I was hoping that maybe you would teach me how to ride."

Chloe thought of Levi. He'd never suggest – or approve, even – of Chloe teaching a *maedel* to ride a horse. But Levi was gone now, and Saul didn't seem to have any qualms about his daughter learning to ride. She eyed Saul. "You approve of this?"

"Of course. I think it would be great for her to learn to ride." He raised a brow. "You do still enjoy riding, don't you?"

"Well, *jah*." Chloe realized that Levi and Saul were like night and day. It seemed uncanny that she would love both of them so much. She thought of all the time alone she and Amanda Chloe would be spending together. This seemed like the perfect solution. She turned to Saul's daughter. "I'd love to, Amanda. Is it all right if I just call you Amanda?"

Amanda Chloe looked to her father for approval, then nodded. "Thank you, Chloe!"

Chloe had never seen the girl so excited. If she loved horses this much, Chloe was certain they'd get along wonderfully.

TWENTY-THREE

*S*aul finally found the phone number he'd been search-
ing for over the last thirty minutes. He'd nearly given
up hope of finding it until he thought to look in Sarah's Bible.
He wondered if Truda knew how much of an impact she'd had
on Sarah's life. And his, although he'd only seen the woman
twice.

As a matter of fact, he never thought he'd want to see her
again. He'd consciously blamed her many times for ruining his
and Sarah's relationship and causing them to be shunned from
their community. But now that Saul's eyes were open, he could
see clearly. He now recognized Truda for who she was: a mes-
senger from God. Not an angel or anything, but one with beautiful feet. He thought of the Bible verse he'd read recently, *How
beautiful are the feet of them that preach the gospel of peace,
and bring glad tidings of good things!* At the time, he had no
idea he was actually fighting *against* the will of the Lord. Life
could definitely be perplexing at times.

Chloe led the way to the barn with Amanda close behind. Saul hadn't told her much about Amanda's experience with horses, but she guessed the girl couldn't be too familiar with them if she didn't know how to ride.

"How old are you?" Chloe could probably figure the answer easily in her head, but she wanted to strike up a conversation with Amanda. Besides, she had no desire to reopen old wounds. Just seeing Saul did enough of that.

"Ten."

Chloe had noticed that Amanda seemed to be a quiet type. The girl reminded her of Levi; he had always been quiet, steady, and secure. Chloe wondered if, perhaps, the girl took after her mother. "Have you been on a horse before?"

"Just with *Dat* when I was little. Not by myself, though."

"Did your *mamm* like horses?" Chloe reached out to stroke one of the mares.

Amanda shrugged. "I don't really know. I was closer to *Dat*. *Mamm* was in the *Bann*. Most folks thought I shouldn't spend much time with her. They said she believed crazy things – mostly my *grossdawdi*. I guess he didn't want me to learn her worldly ways."

Chloe's heart lurched. *Her grandfather told her that her* mamm *was* ferhoodled *and worldly because she believed the Truth? Bishop or no, how could he say such things about his own flesh and blood daughter?* She couldn't imagine her own father-in-law, Bishop Hostettler, ever saying something like that. What kind of hardships had this family gone through? "I'm sorry, Amanda. You must miss your *mamm*."

"I guess so." She sighed. "*Dat* does a *gut* job with us, I think. We don't really need a *mamm*."

Oh, yes, you do. Chloe frowned. Did this mean that Amanda didn't want her in their lives? "Amanda, how do you feel about your father and me?"

She shifted from one foot to the other, then stared at the horses. "I thought we were going to ride horses."

"We are. Let's get them saddled up." It was clear Amanda didn't want to talk, so Chloe decided to tackle that subject later – if at all. She and Saul should probably have a talk about their *kinner.* Chloe had the distinct feeling that Amanda thought she was trying to steal her father away. She hoped Amanda could see that she was actually attempting to fill the missing pieces to the puzzle: a mother for Saul's children and a father for her own. And, of course, a spouse for each of them.

She knew God was the ultimate healer of broken hearts. Hopefully, He would mend all their hearts together into one loving family. *Jah*, Chloe would have to pray for that.

"How did Amanda Chloe's riding lesson go today?" Saul bent down and kissed Chloe's cheek. He glanced around the living room. "Are the *kinner* playing outside?"

"*Jah.*" Chloe tapped her foot. Amanda's riding lesson had gone well, but Chloe had no intention of discussing *that* event until she and Saul settled some things; they had a thing or two to discuss. She'd been stewing on Amanda's words from earlier this morning. "Shunning or no, promise me that you'll never do that to our family, Saul."

Saul stared at Chloe in confusion. "Do what?"

"Tear our family apart. I couldn't bear being separated from my children."

Saul rubbed his forehead. "Wait a minute. Where did all this come from? What is this about? What did I do?"

"Sarah. The shunning. I don't understand, Saul. Why – how could you do Bishop Mast's bidding like that? To keep a child from her mother has to be one of the cruelest things there is."

"What happened today?" Saul frowned.

"It seems like Amanda barely even knew her mother. She said that she spent most of her time with you or her grandparents."

"She did. Sarah was in the *Bann.*"

"I understand that. What I don't understand is *you.* How could you deny *your wife* time with her *own* daughter? How could you deprive your daughter out of a relationship with her mother?" Chloe's incredulous voice rose. "Don't you think children, especially girls, *need* their mother?"

Saul raised his shoulders, then released a long sigh. "I thought I was doing the right thing."

"How could you believe that was the right thing?"

"That's what I was told to do. The leaders didn't want Sarah to have much contact with anyone from our community, including her own daughter. They said that if we shunned her, maybe she would miss us enough to renounce the foolishness that she'd come to believe, and repent. I'd hoped that she would. I'd prayed that she would. It never happened."

Chloe shook her head in disbelief.

Saul stepped near and stroked her arm. "Chloe, I'd give anything to be able to go back and ask Sarah's forgiveness. I realize that what we did was wrong, but that was our way. That's how things are done. And no, I won't ever do anything like that again. You have my promise."

Chloe stepped back. "How can I know for sure?"

"You'll just have to trust me. I can only give you my word." Saul blew out another breath. "I don't know what else I can say. Chloe, you have to understand that Bishop Mast's district is different than yours."

"So, what about your *kinner*? Our *kinner*. Will your folks not be able to see them? How about Sarah's folks?" Chloe paced back and forth between the couch and the wall. "I really think we need to take all these things into consideration."

"You're right. I don't know how my folks will react. They felt sorry for Sarah when she was in the *Bann*. I know my mother ached to spend time with her, but didn't for fear of the consequences. When I was in the *Bann* too, my folks didn't visit us. As for Sarah's folks, I'm sure they won't have anything to do with us." He reached a hand to Chloe and she hesitantly grasped it. "Listen, Chloe. We can't control what others do, that is between them and God. We can only do what we think is right according to God's Word. When we marry, you will be living with a shunned man. It's not going to be an easy road, but with God's help, I know we'll be able to get through whatever comes our way."

"I just feel so bad. Like I'm tearing your *kinner* away from their *grosseldre*."

"*They* are choosing to shun *us*. It's not the other way around. And whether we marry or not, I've already trusted Christ. The only way to avoid the *Bann* is to renounce my faith in Christ and I'm not going to do that. I finally understand why Sarah was so steadfast in her beliefs. There are just some things that are more important than peace in the family. Remember, Jesus said, '*I come not to bring peace, but a sword.*'"

Chloe nodded. "I wish it didn't have to be this difficult."

"Let's just pray about this Chloe. If the king's heart is in the hand of the Lord, I think He's probably got our children's grandparents' hearts too, *jah*?"

Chloe offered a half-smile. "*Jah.* We will pray and trust *Der Herr.*"

"Besides, your folks and the Hostettlers will welcome them with open arms, I'm guessing."

Chloe smiled. "You're right. They will love *all* our children as though they are their own."

Saul opened his arms to Chloe and she gladly entered his embrace now. "We can do this, Chloe. God will help us."

TWENTY-FOUR

*C*hloe opened the door to the cookstove and checked on the casserole. She peeked out the back door when she heard a noise, hoping perchance Saul had stopped by. It had been nearly two weeks since she'd last seen Saul and her heart yearned for his presence. He'd been working overtime so they could have some extra money to take a short honeymoon to Ocean City. Her folks had offered to watch the *kinner* for them while they were gone. She could hardly wait.

Just two more months and she and Saul would be husband and wife. Exciting, *jah*, but the event would be bittersweet. It would mark the one year anniversary of her beloved Levi's passing. Her heart would always ache for him, she lamented, but life had to move on.

Hannah was still enamored with her 'new *dat*', as she called him. Evidence of Saul's love for her children shone every time he was near them. Chloe's heart soared at the thought of him being the *kinner's* father. Clearly, he would be a *gut dat*.

Only one thing worried Chloe about their union: Amanda Chloe. Despite their bi-weekly riding lessons, Amanda still hadn't opened up. Nor had she softened toward Chloe. Saul didn't seem worried about it. He figured she'd come around eventually. Chloe hoped he was right.

Another potential problem was her brother, Stephen. He'd strongly suggested that she steer clear of Saul. Several times. Chloe reminded her brother that she was a grown woman, capable of making her own decisions. But that hadn't prevented Stephen from confronting Saul. Twice. It seemed Stephen couldn't let the past lie; he still didn't trust Saul.

Chloe's heart leaped when the sound of buggy wheels drew her attention again to the window. When she opened the door, she was surprised, and a little disappointed, to see Bishop Hostettler.

"Good evening, *dochder*," Judah greeted.

"Hello, Judah. What brings you by tonight?" Chloe's smiled faded when she noticed Judah's frown.

"I'm afraid I have some not so *gut* news. Can we take a seat in the *schtupp*?" He said warily.

Chloe's mind raced. *What could be wrong? Did somebody die?* Before she decided to panic, she told herself she would listen to what Judah had to say. "Is something wrong?"

"Are *mei kinskinner* here?" He surveyed the room.

"I sent them upstairs to play until supper."

"*Gut*. It is best if they don't hear this."

Hear what? What could be so bad that the children couldn't hear? Her heart quickened.

"It's about Saul."

Chloe's eyes widened. *No, not Saul! Anyone but Saul. Please, God.*

"I don't really know how to put this, so I'll just come out and say it." Judah blew out a heavy breath. "He's been cheating on you."

"What?" Chloe shook her head. "No. I don't believe it. It can't be true."

"I'm sorry, *dochder*. I'm afraid it is. He was seen having dinner with a young woman. They were engaged in more intimate behavior as well."

Chloe's eyes filled with tears. "When?"

"Just last night. I'm sorry. I wish it weren't true. But I guess it is better that you found out now instead of after you married. I'm afraid marrying him might have been the biggest mistake you'd ever make." He placed a hand on her shoulder. "Listen, Chloe. I know you are grieved by this. But you do not have to marry right away to have a *daed* for the *kinner*. The community will give you all the help you need."

Chloe sat in shock as Judah's words continued to register. *The community?* Could the community provide the easy companionship a husband would? Or the warm body to sleep next to on cold nights? Or the strong arms to hold her when she cried? Or more children…*kinner* that resembled both her and Saul?

Chloe ran from the living room and into her bedroom. She sobbed into her pillow, not caring whether Judah was there and watching or not. *Why? Why, God? How could you let this happen?* Stephen had been right all along. Saul wasn't trustworthy.

She didn't want to believe it, but as she thought of recent events, things started adding up. Like Saul not calling all week. Working overtime. Ever since he'd cancelled their last date… Oh, how was she going to break this news to the girls? The poor *maed* had already lost so much. Hannah, especially, would be devastated.

When Chloe heard Judah's buggy rumbling back out of the driveway, she forced herself out of bed. After quickly giving the girls their supper, sending them to bed early, and nursing Levi, Chloe retired for the evening and cried herself to sleep for what seemed to be the millionth time.

The following morning, Chloe had baked six loaves of bread, cleaned the house from top to bottom, and was currently working in the garden. She had to do anything and everything to keep her mind off Saul.

Her mouth now draped open. Was that Saul's buggy driving up the lane? What nerve! And he wasn't alone. He'd brought all of his children with him. Did he expect her to still give Amanda riding lessons? Chloe glanced up and he threw up a friendly wave. She scowled in response. When he noticed Chloe in the garden on the side of the barn, he sent the children into the house, and strode toward her.

Chloe took a deep breath and dusted off her hands before she approached Saul. She felt like slapping him across the face, but she wouldn't. He would stand there and listen to what she had to say whether he liked it or not. And boy, did she have something to say.

"Good morning, beautiful!" Saul's eyes sparkled.

How dare he! "I believed you the first time, Saul Brenneman, when I was fourteen. I didn't think you'd cheated on me but others had said you had. I didn't believe them, but it seems I was wrong. And now, I can't believe you're doing it again." Chloe couldn't help it when the tears formed in her eyes. "Is this the real reason you were shunned, Saul? Did you cheat on Sarah, too?"

Saul frowned. "Wha – cheat on Sarah? No. No, Chloe, I didn't cheat on Sarah. And I didn't – I wouldn't – cheat on you, either!" Saul raked a hand through his hair. "I don't know why you're saying this, Chloe. What makes you think I've been seeing someone else?"

"Judah told me. And I'm glad that I found out now instead of after we married. My children have been through enough already with their father dying."

"Chloe, I–"

"Will you please just go, Saul? It'll be easier for everyone if you just go. I don't want to hear any excuses."

Saul grasped both of her arms and searched her eyes. "No, I will *not* go. You have to hear me out. Chloe, I'm not seeing anyone else. I don't love anyone else. I only love you."

Why did he insist on acting like this? Chloe rolled her eyes. He put all those actors in Hollywood to shame.

"Take your hands off her," a voice boomed from behind him.

Chloe was somewhat relieved when her brother showed up.

"No. She has to hear my side. I'm not leaving until she hears what I have to say," Saul declared.

"I said to take your hands off my sister. Now." Stephen reached for Saul's wrists to force his grip off Chloe's arms. Saul reluctantly released Chloe, shrugging Stephen off.

"This conversation is between me and Chloe. You need to go, Stephen."

"If I heard my sister correctly, she asked *you* to go. Now I suggest you go back home to your own district where you belong."

"I'm not going anywhere." Saul stood his ground. He turned back to Chloe. "Please believe me, Chloe. I don't know what you heard when we were courting, but it wasn't true. I didn't want to have anything to do with Sarah or the baby. In fact, I resented both of them. They were the reason *we* couldn't be together. I even accused Sarah of getting pregnant on purpose." Saul turned when he thought he'd heard a noise inside the barn, then quickly refocused his attention. "I had to *learn* to love Sarah, but loving you always came naturally."

Saul's adamancy was nearly enough to persuade her current volatile emotions. Chloe wanted to believe him, she yearned to believe him. "What about the woman?"

Saul raised his palms. "What woman? I honestly have no idea what you're talking about."

"I can't believe you're denying this." Stephen frowned and shook his head. "Chloe, I saw him with my own two eyes."

"Saw what?" Saul seemed more exasperated by the minute.

"You and the *Englisch* woman. At the restaurant. Does that refresh your memory at all?" Stephen spoke to Saul as though he were an eight-year-old.

"Truda?" Saul's brow raised. "You think that Truda and I—" Saul chuckled. "Truda was a *gut* friend of Sarah's."

Stephen's arms crossed his chest. "I saw the two of you holding hands...and she was in your arms."

Saul glowered at Stephen. "We were talking about my *fraa*. Truda had led Sarah to the Lord and I thanked her for it. She and Sarah met together for years and prayed that I'd get saved someday. I told her about the note Sarah left. Sarah had asked *Der Herr* to do whatever it takes for me to find Jesus. Unfortunately, that meant losing my *fraa*." Saul pivoted toward Chloe. "I also told Truda that I'd found another woman to marry, one that I'd known and courted many years ago. One that I love." Saul's eyes locked with Chloe's, conveying the love he exuded. "Chloe, I have *never* had any romantic interest in Truda, or *anyone* else, for that matter. I've never once cheated on you. I love you and I want to be with you more than anything in this world."

Saul is *innocent!*

Stephen looked at Chloe. "Do you believe this?"

She nodded. "Yes, I do." Saul reached his hand out to her and she grasped it. "I'm sorry for doubting you, Saul." Chloe frowned.

Stephen threw his hands up and walked toward the house.

Saul pulled Chloe near, her ear pressed against his pounding heart. "Doubt me if you must, but don't ever leave me, Chloe." His lips pressed the top of her prayer kapp and he closed his eyes. "Please, don't ever leave me."

TWENTY-FIVE

*S*aul looked down at the hand tugging on his pocket. "Timothy? What are you doing out here? I'm certain sure I told you *kinner* to play inside until *after* dinner." He released Chloe from his embrace and frowned at his oldest son.

"Dinner's been on the table for ten minutes already. Amanda Chloe was supposed to come out and get ya," the boy said.

"I haven't seen Amanda Chloe. We were having a discussion."

"Looked like you was kissin' to me."

Saul blew out a breath and shook his head. "That's none of your business."

"Really, *Dat*. I ain't seen her since she come out here," Timothy insisted.

"She probably went back into the house. Why don't you go check? She might be holding the *boppli* or playing with Lyddie in the girls' room."

Timothy shook his head adamantly. "Nope. Hannah's holding the *boppli*–"

Chloe gasped, then immediately ran toward the house.

"What'd she do that for?" Timothy asked, staring at the door Chloe had just burst through.

"Because that's what *mamms* do. Hannah's a little young to be holding the *boppli* on her own. Babies need to be held a certain way, and they can get hurt really bad if they're dropped," Saul explained. He playfully tousled Timothy's blond hair. "*Kumm*, let's go have some dinner."

"But what about Amanda Chloe?"

"I'm sure she's inside, but I'll check the barn just in case."

"Can I come with ya, *Dat*?" The boy asked eagerly.

"*Jah, kumm*." Saul paced to the barn door, but it swung wide open on its own. "*Ach*, Stephen. I didn't realize you were still here." Saul frowned. Hopefully, Chloe's brother didn't have any *more* trouble to stir up.

Stephen hung his head, then lifted his eyes to Saul's.

Saul noticed Stephen's hat near a bale of hay and realized he must've been praying.

"I think I owe you an apology."

Stephen's apologizing? Will wonders never cease!

"I misjudged you, Saul. I hope you'll forgive me."

Saul reached for his outstretched hand and offered a firm shake. "All is forgiven."

"Saul?"

He turned at the sound of Chloe's voice. She carried a snuggly-wrapped little Levi in her arms. "Is Amanda out here? I couldn't find her in the house." She frowned.

"See? Told you," Timothy interjected. "I couldn't find her neither."

"The barn door was open when I came in," Stephen added. "Do you think she may be up in the haymow?"

Saul deftly climbed the ladder to the large second story. "Amanda Chloe? Are you up here?"

Silence.

"Saul, one of the horses is gone!" Chloe exclaimed. "She didn't take the saddle either. They're both still here."

He bolted back down the ladder. "Why would she have gone off by herself? And without a saddle?" Saul raised his hat and ran a hand through his hair. "It doesn't make sense."

"She's never ridden bareback. It's very dangerous." Chloe's eyes met Saul's, communicating her concern.

Stephen grimaced. "Do you suppose she overheard us talking?"

"Oh no!" Chloe worriedly glanced out the door's opening. "This isn't good, Saul."

"Let's go," Stephen offered. "I'll help you find her. Chloe, if Saul and I aren't back in thirty minutes, ring the bell."

Chloe nodded.

Saul and Stephen quickly saddled their horses, then rode off in search of Amanda Chloe. *Dear Lord, please keep my daughter safe. Help us find her quickly. Show us where to go,* he breathed the silent prayer.

Before Saul and Stephen even made it out of Chloe's long driveway, they spotted a mare. Stephen's jaw clenched. Where was the girl? He surveyed the woods nearby, hoping for a glimpse of Amanda Chloe.

"That looks like Chloe's horse." Stephen pointed. "She probably went for a walk in the woods," he said, attempting to sound hopeful.

Saul nodded quietly, but Stephen read the fear in his eyes.

"Let's check it out," Stephen suggested.

The two men neared the horse and Stephen approached it cautiously. He didn't want to scare the mare off. He spoke softly to the creature while adroitly ringing a rope around her neck. Stephen hastily tethered the other end of the rope to a tree.

"Oh no."

Stephen grimaced when he heard Saul's moan. He raced to Saul, some twenty feet away, and crouched next to him. His eyes swept over Amanda Chloe's body for injuries, but her mangled leg wasn't easy to miss.

Saul's shaky hand gently stroked his daughter's brow as she lay unconscious between two trees. He looked up at Stephen helplessly.

"I'll go call an ambulance."

Stephen chided himself as he swiftly rode back toward Chloe's barn. If he hadn't confronted Saul in the first place, this never would have happened. *Dear God, please let Saul's daughter make it.* He determined then and there he would pay for all her hospital expenses. *And funeral, if necessary,* he thought ashamedly.

The ominous beep of a heart monitor from a room down the hall grated on Saul's nerves; he felt like ripping the stupid thing off the wall. And carrying his daughter out of this wretched place. It had been over an hour and he still hadn't received any word about Amanda Chloe's condition. He feared it wasn't good. He bowed his head once again, praying that she'd be okay.

At first sight of his daughter, the medical team decided she required immediate surgery. The doctor had informed him that Amanda Chloe's leg might need to be amputated. He prayed that it wouldn't. How would she react if she woke up without one of her legs? Even the thought was disturbing. Saul anxiously paced the waiting room.

"*Kumm,* sit down," Chloe beckoned, her voice sympathetic. When he continued to pace, she walked to him and placed a calming hand on his arm.

Saul wrapped his arms around his beloved and held her tight, alleviating a smidgen of his tension. "I'm so thankful you're here with me, Chloe."

Her eyes met his. "Where else would I be?"

He unwillingly released her when more visitors filed into the waiting room. Saul had never been long on patience and all this waiting was killing him. He and Chloe took a seat, when he noticed a tear slip down her cheek. Saul grasped her hand. "She's going to be alright." He hoped his words were true.

"This is all my fault. I shouldn't have taught her to ride. If I hadn't, she never would have gotten on that horse." She wiped a tear away with a shaky hand.

Saul's brow lowered and he raised her chin. "Chloe, don't you go thinking any of this is your fault. *I* asked you to teach her to ride."

She shook her head. "I should have listened to Levi. He was right."

"Right about what?"

"About *maed* riding horses. He said it wasn't proper and he always worried about me when I would ride. If I'd honored his wishes, Amanda Chloe wouldn't be in that operating room."

"That's nonsense, Chloe. There's nothing wrong with anyone riding horses, male or female. And this has nothing to do with that. We have no way of knowing the future. You, nor I, knew that Amanda was going to try to ride bareback. We can't be by our children's sides every second of the day and prevent every possible disaster. We have to place them in God's hands and trust Him with whatever happens. God could have prevented the accident but for some reason, He didn't."

Chloe nodded silently, but Saul guessed that she still blamed herself. He wished they could just kiss away all their fears and trials, but that was not possible. They would just have to trust *Der Herr*, because with God, all things were possible.

Saul and Chloe entered Amanda's hospital room, somewhat relieved at the news the orthopedic surgeon delivered. Amanda's leg was still intact, although not in the best shape. She'd wear a cast for six to eight weeks, and hope that the leg healed properly. Because of the injuries sustained and Amanda's age, they did their best to try to save it. Only time would tell whether their efforts were fruitful.

Chloe glanced at Saul, then at Amanda. The girl grimaced when she caught sight of her father. Saul neared his daughter's bed and took her hand, a concerned frown formed on his face.

"Amanda Chloe, how are you feeling?" Saul asked.

She shrugged. "Okay, I guess. My leg hurts some."

"Do you remember what happened?" Saul's brow raised.

Amanda nodded. "I was riding the horse."

"Why?"

She briefly looked up at Chloe, then stared at her folded cast. "I was mad."

"Mad? Why?"

"You don't want me. All you want is *her*. You didn't even care for me or *Mamm*."

"Wha– that's not true, Amanda Chloe. I loved you and your *mudder* very much." Chloe detected the distress in Saul voice.

Amanda pointed a finger at Saul. "That's not what you said! You said you didn't want me or *Mamm*. I heard you."

"You heard me out of context. Yes, I thought some things that I shouldn't have. Your *mamm* and I were very young and we didn't know what we were doing. I can explain more about that when you're older. But don't think that I didn't love you and *Mamm*."

Amanda Chloe shrugged.

Saul lifted her chin. "Look at me, Amanda. I am your father; I love you. Chloe loves you, too." Chloe nodded in confirmation. "She is going to be your new *mamm*. I was wrong by keeping you away from your mother before. Chloe helped me to see that. She showed me that you do need a mother."

Chloe spoke up. "I'm sorry if I did or said something to make you upset."

Amanda's chin quivered. "I miss *Mamm*." She wiped away a tear.

Saul now sat on the bed and drew his daughter's head to his chest. "I know you do. We all do." The sight struck a chord on Chloe's heartstrings and she had to momentarily turn away to gather her emotions.

Chloe inched forward. "Amanda, I hope you don't feel like I'm trying to take your mother's place. Nobody can do that. I don't want you to forget your mother. You may talk about her any time. Okay?"

Amanda wiped another tear from her cheek and nodded. "Okay. *Denki*, Chloe."

Saul surveyed his daughter's wounded leg. "Next time you need to talk to someone, please don't run off." He gestured to the hospital bed. "This could have been prevented."

Amanda nodded sheepishly.

TWENTY-SIX

"*Elbedritschel* hunting?" Ruthie's beau, Ethan, scratched his head. "What on earth is *elba*-whatever hunting?"

Saul glanced around at the others in the barn. He wasn't touching this one.

"You've never heard of *Elbedritschel*?" Judah Hostettler rubbed his beard.

Ethan shook his head.

Jonathan Fisher's eyes widened. "Best eatin' that ever was! Especially in a stew. You bring some *Elbedritschel* home to Ruthie and I guarantee you you'll get a kiss you'll never forget."

Judah cleared his throat.

"After you're married, that is." Jonathan smirked.

Judah explained. "The *Elbedritschel* is a small animal, 'bout the size of a rabbit, I'd say. They're not too easy to catch, though. We don't use guns for catchin' 'um because they're best fresh. A dead *Elbedritschel*, even if it's just an hour-old kill, will taste worse than a skunk. But fresh, oh boy! There's nothin' like it."

Ethan licked his lips.

"Saul, did you bring the gunny sack?" Jonathan asked.

Saul nodded and held up the empty burlap bag.

"You know, I think maybe Ethan here would probably prefer something easy, like deer hunting. *Elbedritschel* will be too difficult for a first hunt, I think," Judah said.

"Oh no. We can go *Elbedritschel* hunting," Ethan asserted. "Besides, I want to see the look on Ruthie's face."

"*Jah*, so do I," Jonathan agreed.

Saul smiled and followed the others out the barn door.

Saul and the others walked through a large wooded area until they came to a vast meadow. Darkness had descended upon the land several hours ago and the creatures of the forest were beginning to make their appearances. Judah had led the way with the flash light, then came to an abrupt stop.

He whispered the instructions to all. "Okay, Ethan, here's what we do. You are going to wait right here with the gunny sack. Jonathan, Saul, and I will go behind the trees out yonder." He pointed to three different trees around the perimeter of the meadow. "When we see the *Elbedritschel*, we will drive him out into the meadow. You come running as fast as you can and scoop him up into the bag. Do you think you can handle that?"

Ethan rubbed his hands together and smiled. "Yeah, sure."

"Here, I'll leave the flashlight with you," Judah offered.

Saul and the others each set off toward their destinations, while Ethan stayed behind his assigned tree and waited.

Chloe turned when she heard footsteps rubbing on the back steps. She smiled when Ruthie walked through the door.

"How did Ethan's hunting trip go with the guys?" Chloe asked. "I haven't heard anything from Saul yet."

Ruthie shook her head. "I haven't heard anything either. What time did Saul say they'd be back?"

"Sometime this morning. That's why I'm making breakfast."

"Smells good. I can't wait to see Ethan. I haven't seen him for a couple of days." Ruthie's eyes sparkled. "Just two more weeks and we'll be married!"

"It's exciting, isn't it?" She opened the door to the cookstove to check on her breakfast casserole.

Ruthie nodded. "You're next."

Chloe frowned.

"What's wrong?"

"It's different getting married the second time. Don't get me wrong. I love Saul and I'm excited that we'll be married soon, but I feel like I'm losing something. I know Levi is never coming back. It's just…oh, I don't know. It seems like I'm closing one book of my life – one that I'll never be able to reopen again – and opening another."

"It's bittersweet, *jah*?" Ruthie half-smiled.

Chloe nodded. "I guess that would be the right word."

Ruthie spun around at the sound of the turning door handle. "Look who's here!" She pulled the door open for the men and they clambered through the doorway. She stuck her head outside and surveyed the property. "Where's Ethan?"

The men looked at each other and shrugged. "Don't know. Isn't he here?" Jonathan asked.

"He was supposed to be with you," Ruthie said.

"I'm sure he'll show up." Saul neared Chloe and rubbed her arm. She read the desire in his eyes, but knew he'd abstained from kissing her because of their company. "Is breakfast ready?"

"*Jah.* Ruthie, will you set the table?"

Saul took a bite of the delicious breakfast casserole Chloe'd made and gave thanks once again for his good fortune. He wished he could stay and spend all day with her, and night, he admitted, but that wouldn't happen for a couple of months yet. Until then, he'd just have to be patient.

Ruthie brightened, as though she'd just been struck with an idea. "Hey, now that you've joined our district, you're not blind Saul anymore!"

"That's right. God opened my eyes and now I can see." Saul wondered, had his eyes been opened sooner, if Sarah would still be alive. A part of him wished it were so, but then he wouldn't have gotten a second chance with Chloe...He was just glad that

God was the one in charge and he didn't have to make all the big decisions. "So, should I change my name to Paul now?"

Ruthie shook her head. "I don't think so. That would be too confusing. Besides, you look like a Saul."

Ruthie abruptly jumped up from the table before anyone else heard a sound. Saul and the others turned when she came into the dining area with Ethan beside her.

Ethan yawned. "Sorry, I didn't come back with you. I must've fallen asleep out there."

Ruthie's eyes widened. "You've been out there all this time?"

Ethan nodded. "Did anyone end up catching one?"

Jonathan shook his head, grinning. "Nope. We headed home about a half hour after we left you."

"A half hour?" Ethan scratched his head in confusion.

Ruthie's hand planted on her hip. "Wait a minute. What were you hunting for?"

"Some elder brittle or something," Ethan said shrugging.

Ruthie glared at Jonathan, Bishop Hostettler, and Saul. She tiptoed up to Ethan's ear and whispered, "The *Elbedritschel* doesn't exist."

Ethan's jaw dropped. "But I-" A look of frustration crossed his face, then he glanced at the amused faces around the table. Suddenly, he burst into uncontrollable laughter and the others joined in as well.

When they'd all finally gained their composure, Ruthie asked, "So, where have you all been?"

Judah answered, "We went and stayed at Jonathan and Susanna's house. The Fishers had nice warm comfy beds for us to sleep in." His eyes sparkled.

EPILOGUE

*S*aul glanced to his beloved sitting on the chair next to him. Never in a million years would he have thought this day would come. But it had. Here he and Chloe were, now standing in front of Bishop Hostettler and the congregation of Paradise, ready to say the vows that would join them together as one for the remainder of their lives.

He searched the women's side of the room and spotted all three of his *dochdern* and little Levi in the back with their *grossmudder* Mary Esh and newlywed Ruthie Spencer. He smiled when Amanda Chloe and Hannah both waved. His eyes meandered to the opposite side of the congregation and he spotted his sons with their new *grossdawdi* Peter Esh.

He'd hoped his folks would show but they hadn't. His mother did manage to send him a letter wishing him the best with his new family. She said she and his father offered daily prayers for them. She'd also enclosed five hundred dollars, no doubt a gift from his father. Saul was certain sure Bishop Mast wasn't privy to their gift.

A dull pain clenched his heart, but it released the moment he looked into Chloe's tear-filled emerald eyes. Hopefully, they'd be blessed with a *boppli* this time next year. They'd already picked out a name for a baby, should they have a *maedel*: Rachel Sarah Brenneman. Chloe had insisted on Sarah as the middle name, just as Sarah had insisted on Amanda Chloe's middle name.

Saul realized he had to be the most blessed man that ever lived to have had the opportunity to be married to two of the finest women God had ever made. No, he hadn't known it the whole time, but now he knew he could trust God. When he had been making a mess of his life, ignoring God's will and doing his own thing, God had been patiently walking behind him and picking up all the broken threads he'd left in his wake. Now, God had wrought together a tapestry of love more beautiful than Saul ever could have imagined.

Saul set his fork down when he noticed Hannah approaching the table. They'd wanted all their children in attendance at the wedding and dinner reception. This was a day of celebration for the whole family.

Hannah climbed up into the lap of her new *dat*. "Do ya fink my fiwst *dat* and Mandy's fiwst *mamm* knows each other in Heaben?"

Saul smiled. "I suppose so."

"Do ya fink they gots mawied too, like you and *Mamm*?"

Saul shook his head. "*Nee*, I don't think so."

Hannah nodded adamantly. "Uh huh! They have to 'cause Mandy's *mamm* would be sad like *Mamm* was afore she mawied you."

Saul raised a brow to Chloe and she returned an amused smile. "I don't think she's sad. She's with Jesus now."

"And being in Heaben wif Jesus is the best place in the whole wowd, ain't so, *Dat*?"

"That's right, Hannah." He kissed the top of her prayer *kapp*. "Being with Jesus is the best place in the world."

The End

Amish Girls Holiday

A
Christmas
of Mercy

J.E.B. Spredemann

A Christmas of Mercy

(An Amish Girls Holiday Novella)

As Christmas draws near, Katrina Thompson looks forward to the birth of her first grandchild. But when the blessed event digs up the discovery of her buried criminal past, Officer Love feels duty-bound to report the wrongdoing. The Amish community of Paradise has long since forgiven Katrina for her past mistakes, but will she receive mercy at the hands of the law?

CPSIA information can be obtained at www.ICGtesting.com
Printed in the USA
BVOW08s1105270915

419839BV00003B/119/P